Divine Submission

Book Three:

The Realm of Echoes

Chapter One-Hundred-Fifty-Two: The Mirror Forgot to Lie (Rewrite)

The air in the Realm of Echoes didn't breathe.

It pulsed.

Every breath Medusa took pressed against her skin like a whispered truth she hadn't asked to remember. The ground shimmered underfoot, mirror, not marble, reflecting not just her body, but every version of herself the gods had ever tried to shape or shatter.

She stepped forward, barefoot, serpents quiet beneath her hair.

Behind her, the mirror gateway rippled closed with a hush, leaving only Andreas.

His presence burned at her back before he touched her. He didn't speak. He didn't need to. This Realm wasn't built for words; it was built for reflection. And the silence between them stretched taut like silk before the snap.

Medusa stared into a mirror on her left.

In it, she wore chains made of celestial gold and a crown she hadn't chosen.

In the next, she ruled alone, her throne surrounded by statues of gods who had dared to cross her.

And in the third...

She was on her knees.

Naked. Crownless. Consumed.

Andreas's reflection hovered just behind her in that one. His fire ran like veins beneath his skin; his gaze fixed on her like she was the only myth he believed in.

She looked away.

Too late.

Andreas was already watching the same reflection. He stepped closer, hand finding the bare curve of her waist.

"You don't trust this place," he said softly.

"I don't trust what it shows me."

His fingers splayed wider. "Then look at me instead."

Chapter One-Hundred-Fifty-Three: The Version That Shouldn't Be

The Realm of Echoes was no longer still.

The mirror that once shimmered with Medusa's desires now pulsed with something darker. Not lust. Not prophecy. Power twisted through memory and malice.

Andreas stood beside her, fire threading over his knuckles, gaze locked on the glass that refused to lie.

And then she stepped through.

A figure. Real. Whole. Not shadow, not reflection. She moved like sovereignty itself, like a queen who had never knelt, never begged, never burned.

She wore Medusa's face.

But not her fire.

This Medusa was draped in ash-coloured silk that didn't whisper, it commanded. Her serpents were bound in golden rings, motionless, coiled like a crown of judgment. Her eyes sharp as shattered vows.

"So," she said, gaze sweeping over Medusa and Andreas with the cold precision of a verdict. "This is what I could have been. Unchosen. Undone. Unbroken in all the wrong ways."

Andreas stepped forward, fire rising in warning. But Medusa lifted a hand.

"She's not here to fight," Medusa said softly. "She's here to replace."

The echo smiled. Not cruel. Certain.

"Correct. You fell. You chose fire. Chaos. Love."
Her eyes grazed Andreas like a knife. "I chose
rule."

"Without love?" Medusa asked.

"Without need," the echo snapped. "I ruled
Olympus without ever crawling back from ruin.
I am what happens when a goddess remembers
she was divine before she was wronged."

Andreas's flame licked higher. "You're a ghost
wearing a crown."

"And yet," she said, stepping closer, "I'm the
version the gods feared enough to erase."

The mirror behind her flared with light. A
dozen others began to ripple each showing
Medusas that could have been: one
worshipped, one weaponized, one kneeling
beside Zeus himself.

Medusa didn't flinch.

"You're not a threat because you were erased," she said, voice like silk dipped in venom. "You're a threat because you forgot what it cost."

The echo tilted her head.

"This realm listens. Shall we ask it who deserves the throne?"

The ground pulsed.

Andreas stepped beside Medusa. "We don't need its permission."

Medusa reached for his hand, her voice a low promise.

"No. But we'll show it the truth."

All around them, the mirrors began to shimmer again.

And from each one, a different Medusa stepped forward.

Not illusions.

Versions.

Not to fight.

To witness.

To decide.

Because this was no longer a reflection.

It was a reckoning.

Chapter One-Hundred-Fifty-Four: The Crown Without Mercy

The ground did not shake.

It listened.

Stone absorbed silence like breath held too long, and the mirrors lining the Realm of Echoes no longer shimmered, they watched. Every version of Medusa stood in quiet formation, their gowns brushing the floor like whispers of what might have been.

Only the unbroken one moved.

Ash-silk sweeping behind her, she circled like a judge before the condemned.

"You waited too long," she said, voice as calm as cruelty. "You let love unmake you."

"I let it remake me," Medusa replied, stepping forward. "That's what you'll never understand."

Behind her, Andreas said nothing. But his fire curved protectively around them, an oath in motion.

One of the mirrors cracked.

The unbroken Medusa turned toward it. A version stepped forward in chains made of gold, gilded, regal, and weeping.

"The gods adored me," she whispered. "But they carved their names into my spine."

Another version emerged barefoot, cloaked in storm light, her eyes blindfolded by prophecy.

"I tried to save them all," she said. "And they erased me anyway."

Then another kneeling in full armour, sword sheathed in her own blood.

"I knelt. I bled," she said. "And they still feared the day I'd rise."

The unbroken Medusa faltered.

Just once.

And that was enough.

"You were never a crown," Medusa whispered, stepping closer, "You were a cage. Beautiful. Impressive. Empty."

Ash-silk flared like wings.

"And you," the echo hissed, "are just a woman who loved a man enough to fall."

Medusa reached for Andreas's hand again. This time, he didn't offer fire he offered truth.

"I didn't fall," Medusa said, her voice low, sharp, and holy. "I chose."

The Realm pulsed. And the mirrors dozens, maybe hundreds reflected the moment a goddess refused to kneel to herself.

One by one, the other Medusas turned.

Not to the echo.

To her.

The one who burned and still stood.

The one who shattered and still chose love.

The one who ruled with the fire, not instead of it.

The mirrors didn't crack.

They bowed.

And the unbroken Medusa?

She vanished.

Like smoke that never dared to burn.

Interlude: In the Fire That Chose Her

They left the Realm of Echoes behind,

but it did not leave them.

The mirrors had bowed.

The versions had watched.

But only Andreas had touched her like this

as if she wasn't a throne to kneel to,

but a flame to burn beside.

Their sanctuary was nothing but shadow and fire.

A cavern carved by time,

veined with obsidian and warmth.

Andreas didn't speak.

He knelt.

Not to worship

to offer.

His hands came to her waist, not to claim,

but to ask.

And Medusa, still trembling from power she
had not lost but chosen

touched his jaw with the back of her fingers.

"I am not broken," she whispered.

"I know," he said, voice like embers.

"But I need you to know it, too."

When she kissed him, it wasn't gentle.

It was sovereign.

Her hands dragged through his hair, pulling

him up to her mouth,

her teeth grazing his lower lip in punishment

and promise.

Andreas's fire rose instinctively

but when it kissed her skin,

it did not burn.

It worshipped.

It curled around her thighs,

traced the lines of her collarbone,

danced up her spine like devotion reborn in

heat.

She gasped as his mouth followed

from throat to breast, to hipbone to knees,

as if he were writing prayers on the altar of her skin.

"I would burn the world for you," he murmured, voice thick.

She grinned darkly, eyes glowing serpentine gold.

"I already did."

He laughed, low and reverent

and she straddled him with the confidence of a queen and the hunger of a woman who had waited.

Her serpents stirred,

not in warning,

but in approval.

Because Andreas did not look at her like a

weapon or a prophecy.

He looked at her like she was the answer.

Their bodies moved like storm and flame

not rushed, not frantic,

but with the deep, slow ache of sovereignty

remembered.

Every kiss said: You chose this.

Every touch said: You are not alone.

And when she shattered in his arms,

head thrown back, crown slipping sideways,

Andreas whispered the only words that ever

mattered.

"You were never meant to kneel."

"I love you standing."

Chapter One-Hundred-Fifty-Five: The Goddess Who Waited Too Long

Athena felt it before she saw it.

A shift subtle, seismic beneath the marble bones of Olympus.

The weight of something ancient returning.

Not war.

Not prophecy.

Choice.

She stood alone in her temple, hands clasped behind her back, staring into the sacred pool that once reflected order.

Now?

It boiled.

Not with heat. With defiance.

The vision that formed was fragmented, rippling between truths:

- A mirror cracking.

- A serpent crown bowing to no one.

- Andreas's fire wrapped around Medusa like worship.

- Versions of a goddess who had been everything... but erased.

Athena's jaw clenched.

"She was meant to fall," she murmured to herself.

"Not rise."

Behind her, the owls lining the rafters stirred.

A sign.

Even her symbols felt the imbalance.

She paced the length of the chamber slowly, each step echoing like judgment she could not cast.

Medusa had not returned to Olympus.

But Olympus already felt her.

The throne room would pretend they hadn't noticed.

Zeus would pretend he wasn't sweating under his gold.

Hera would smile with teeth.

And the others Ares, Hades, even Persephone would begin to drift.

Worse, to choose.

Athena stopped.

In the centre of her chamber sat a tapestry she had never dared finish.

It bore the shape of a serpent.

Half-coiled.

Half-crowned.

She pulled the golden thread taut between her fingers.

"She's not coming for revenge," Athena whispered.

"She's coming to replace us."

The word made her stomach twist.

Not because it wasn't true.

But because a part of her small, sharp, buried knew she had seen this thread long ago. Had warned them. Had begged them not to curse the girl. Had tried to protect her in her own cold, twisted way.

And now?

Now the goddess of wisdom had waited too long.

And the Realm had chosen fire.

Chapter One-Hundred-Fifty-Six: The Gods Who Felt the Fire

The war room was quiet.

Too quiet.

The kind of quiet that meant everything was about to fall.

Ares paced, armour half-clad, rage barely tucked beneath skin. His blade leaned against the wall, forgotten for the first time in centuries.

"She moved through the Mirror Realm like a goddess," he snarled. "And they bowed."

"Not they," Hades corrected coolly, seated at the long obsidian table. "Versions of herself. That's worse."

Hercules leaned back in his chair, arms folded across his chest, watching both brothers like they were already at war.

"She didn't ask them to bow," Hercules said. "They just did."

Ares turned, eyes gleaming like blood in moonlight.

"Don't tell me you're one of them now."

"I'm not anything," Hercules said, voice low. "But I remember what she looked like before the fall. Before the curse. And now?" He exhaled. "Now she looks like she finally remembers who she is."

The tension thickened.

Hades broke the silence with a slow sip of wine. "She chose Andreas," he said.

Ares scoffed. "She chose weakness."

"No," Hades said, tone silk-edged steel. "She chose power that doesn't come from Olympus."

That shut Ares up for a breath.

Then:

"So, what do we do?" Ares asked.

"Wait for her to come for the throne?"

"She doesn't want the throne," Hercules said.

"She wants the world to know she doesn't need it."

Ares slammed a fist onto the table, the marble cracking beneath.

"She was mine before the fall," he growled.

Hades arched a brow.

"She was never yours. None of us ever had her. That's why she terrifies Olympus. She doesn't belong to it."

The fire in the hearth flickered then surged.

Not from wind.

From warning.

They all felt it.

The Realms were shifting.

The crown had slipped.

And Medusa wasn't just a contender now.

She was a choice.

Hades stood, fixing both his brothers with a look carved from the underworld itself.

"I won't fight her," he said. "I won't kneel, either. But I'll stand with her if it comes to that."

Hercules nodded once. "Same."

Ares didn't move. His jaw flexed. His fists clenched.

But he didn't say no.

Which was dangerous.

Because Ares silent was worse than Ares screaming.

Chapter One-Hundred-Fifty-Seven: The Crown That Would Not Kneel

The Realm of Echoes was silent behind her.

But the weight of it what she'd done, what she'd chosen followed like shadow trailing flame.

Medusa stood at the edge of the cliff overlooking the void between Realms, Andreas's hand still warm in hers. The stars above shimmered in deference, as if the cosmos had paused to watch.

She didn't speak.

Not yet.

Her serpents were still, coiled in contemplation instead of rage. They sensed it too something shifting. Something coming.

Andreas broke the silence first.

"You didn't just win," he said. "You changed the mirror."

Medusa nodded slowly. "The mirror doesn't lie. But it does remember."

She let go of his hand and stepped forward, wind catching the edges of her cloak like wings of ash and gold. The versions of her were gone absorbed back into the realm or into herself, she didn't know.

All she knew was that the version who walked forward now...

was the only one left.

The real one.

Suddenly, a flicker of energy rippled through the air. Not fire. Not prophecy.

A message.

It burned into existence in front of her, a seal etched in divine gold, hovering midair like an accusation.

Olympus.

She didn't touch it.

She didn't need to.

The seal cracked on its own.

And Hera's voice bled through like perfume laced with poison.

Come home, Medusa. The throne room awaits your answer."

Medusa exhaled once, slowly. Her gaze flicked skyward, toward the mountain that exiled her, toward the gods who had once named her monster and now summoned her like a storm they'd tried to ignore.

Andreas stepped beside her, eyes narrowing. "It's a trap."

"Of course," she said calmly.

He glanced sideways. "You're not going."

"I'm going," she said, voice even, deliberate, sovereign. "But not to kneel."

Her serpents stirred, golden eyes glowing. Her magic curled around her like dusk preparing to strike.

"I'm going to remind them," she said softly, "that I didn't rise to ask for a crown."

"I am the crown."

Chapter One-Hundred-Fifty-Eight: The God Who Feared the Silence

The throne room of Olympus had never felt so cold.

And Zeus hated it.

The columns still gleamed with celestial gold. The sky above still broke in divine light. But the air, thick and silent felt like it belonged to someone else now.

Someone uninvited.

Someone returned.

"She won't come," he said, mostly to himself.

But even that lie echoed too loudly.

Across the marble dais, Hera sat like carved stone, lips drawn tight, her gaze fixed on nothing.

Ares stood near the wall, unreadable.

Hades was absent.

And that was a problem.

"Why summon her at all?" Apollo asked, lounging in sunlight like this was a game. "If she's not a threat, let her fade."

"She won't fade," Hera snapped. "She was erased. And now the Realms remember her."

Zeus felt the weight of every word. Not because it surprised him.

Because he knew.

hey had all agreed. Long ago.

Erase the girl, spare the crown.

But now?

Now the girl was the crown.

A scroll burned to life beside his throne, an update from the Watchers. The mirror realm bowed. Versions manifested. Medusa had not fought and still won.

Zeus's fingers clenched the armrest, knuckles white.

"Fire without war," he muttered. "That's the most dangerous kind."

He rose.

"We need control before she arrives. A display of strength."

Hera arched a brow. "And what will you do? Throw lightning at her reflection?"

Zeus didn't answer.

But his storm gathered anyway.

Outside, thunder cracked.

He raised his hand, and across Olympus, the banners shifted every pillar now etched in gold, with his symbol above all.

He would not kneel.

He would not share the sky.

"If she dares walk into this throne room," Zeus growled,

"she will learn the gods still rule Olympus."

But even as he said it...

The silence in the room smiled.

Because Olympus already knew

It wasn't Olympus she was coming to rule.

Interlude: The Storm She Chose to Ride

The storm rolled outside the palace, thunder clawing at the heavens like it wanted to be heard.

But Hera didn't flinch.

She watched Zeus from across the chamber, his shoulders tense, lightning coiling at his fingertips, his mind still lost in Medusa's shadow.

That would not do.

Not tonight.

"You're shaking Olympus again," she said, her voice velvet laced with steel. "Tell me... is it fear or desire that keeps your throne so warm?"

Zeus turned, jaw clenched, storm-eyes glowing.

But Hera had already crossed the floor
barefoot, deliberate, each step echoing through
the chamber like the strike of a queen who
didn't need a crown to be obeyed.

She didn't wait for his answer.

She slid her fingers up his bare chest, tracing
the ancient scars that wrapped across his
ribcage like celestial etchings.

"You forget," she whispered, "before Olympus
was yours... you were mine."

His breath caught just once but that was all she
needed.

Her hand fisted in his hair.

Her mouth met his with thunder.

And the storm shattered.

Zeus kissed like war brutal, claiming, endless.

But Hera didn't yield.

She matched him.

Tongue for tongue.

Clash for clash.

Until they weren't gods, they were elements, colliding in worship and wrath.

She pressed him back into the marble pillar, her teeth dragging down his throat, her thighs locking around his hips.

"Let her come," Hera purred into his ear. "But tonight... you'll scream my name."

Zeus growled, thunder rolling from his throat as he spun her, lifting her effortlessly.

Lightning cracked.

Wind roared.

And Hera smiled as his mouth found her breast like hunger made flesh.

"Show me," she gasped, arching into him. "Remind me why Olympus still obeys you."

He did.

Again.

And again.

Until the storm outside was jealous of the storm inside.

When it was over, Zeus lay spent against her, skin glowing gold with sweat and magic.

And Hera, lips swollen, serpentine satisfied, leaned close.

"Now," she said, stroking his jaw,

"let the girl come. We'll be waiting."

Chapter One-Hundred-Fifty-Nine: The Day Olympus Held Its Breath

The gates of Olympus did not open for her.

They bowed.

The divine marble, enchanted and eternal, peeled apart with a hiss of starlight and memory like even the mountain remembered who she had been.

And who she had become.

Medusa stepped forward slowly, her gown a cascade of midnight silk and serpents, each thread humming with the power of the Realms that had crowned her in mirror fire and choice.

Her feet did not tremble.

Her crown did not tilt.

And when the gods dared look down from their thrones…

She looked up.

Unflinching.

Unapologetic.

Andreas walked at her side, his fire dimmed but ready, his jaw set like he'd already chosen who he'd burn for.

They crossed the threshold into the throne chamber.

Silence.

It stretched like a held breath every god watching, every goddess calculating.

Zeus sat atop his dais, glowing gold and coiled like a storm that had forgotten how to break. Hera beside him, radiant and smug, her scent still clinging to the air like sex and power.

"You came," Zeus said. Not a question. Not a welcome.

"I said I would," Medusa replied. Her voice didn't echo it ruled.

Hera tilted her head. "And what is it you seek, dear girl?"

Medusa smiled.

Not kind.

Not cruel.

Inevitable.

"I don't seek."

Her serpents stirred, eyes glittering. Her magic pulsed.

"I've already been chosen. The Realms saw me. And now... so will you."

A low, slow murmur rippled through the court. Apollo leaned forward. Persephone stiffened. Ares stepped off the wall.

Medusa kept her gaze locked on the throne. "This is not a rebellion," she said. "This is a reminder."

"You erased me. But I returned."

"You cursed me. But I rose."

"You crowned yourselves gods..."

She stepped forward.

"And forgot I was never beneath you."

A wind surged through the chamber. Her serpents lifted. Her power bloomed.

And Olympus?

Held its breath.

Because she had not knelt.

And she never would again.

Chapter One-Hundred-Sixty: The Seeds of Discord

Persephone & Apollo's Point of View

(Alternating)

Persephone

She stood at the edge of the dais; fingers wrapped around her obsidian scepter like it could steady the chaos blooming inside her.

Medusa didn't belong here.

But gods she fit.

That was the danger.

Persephone watched her, burning and bold, serpents draped like jewellery, power crackling like ripened fruit in a garden she'd never been invited to rule.

"She's too loud," Persephone murmured to no one.

Too sure. Too sovereign.

Too… free.

It wasn't jealousy.

(It was.)

It wasn't fear.

(It was.)

It was the knowledge that Medusa didn't need Olympus to stand and that made her more goddess than the rest of them combined.

"She will divide us," Persephone whispered, turning toward Apollo. "She already has."

Apollo

He sat reclined on a sunbeam throne, legs crossed, golden lyre across his lap. His eyes glittered like stars pretending not to blink.

"No," he said, smiling without warmth. "She won't divide us."

He plucked a single note from the lyre.

High. Discordant.

"We will divide us."

The gods were too proud.

Too old.

Too shaken by a girl who walked into their court like she'd built it herself.

Persephone's jaw clenched. "Hades will side with her."

Apollo raised a brow. "As will Hercules."

"Then we isolate her."

He tilted his head.

"Or," he said, voice smooth as nectar laced with knives,

"we make her look like what they all feared she was."

Persephone turned to face him fully, brows raised.

Apollo's smile widened.

"We don't fight the queen," he said.

"We twist the crown."

Chapter One-Hundred-Sixty-One: The Silence Between Serpents

They were watching her.

Not with awe now. Not with fear.

With calculation.

Medusa stood tall beneath Olympus's celestial dome, light pouring down like judgment dressed in gold. The thrones shimmered in their smug glory, but she saw past the glow into the cold rot beneath.

They weren't stunned anymore.

They were deciding.

Andreas stood close, his fire twitching at the edges of his skin. He felt it too.

Persephone's gaze was too smooth.

Apollo's smile too sharp.

Hera smug.

Zeus still.

Only one didn't pretend.

Hades.

He leaned in the shadow of the eastern column, unreadable. Not withdrawn. Not hostile. Just... measuring.

Medusa met his eyes.

He didn't flinch.

He didn't bow.

He did nothing at all.

And that told her everything.

The court's silence was no longer reverent.

It was strategic.

Someone whispered. A breath. A rustle. A step.

Medusa's serpents lifted slightly, scenting
deceit on divine wind.

"You feel that?" Andreas murmured beside her.

"I feel them turning," she replied softly.

"They fear you."

"No," she said, eyes never leaving the thrones.
"They've stopped fearing. Now they're
planning."

Persephone shifted. Apollo twirled a ring on his finger that didn't exist a moment ago.

"They're going to try to make you the villain," Andreas warned.

"Let them," Medusa said.

"I never asked for their story."

She stepped forward, letting her voice ripple through the throne room like silk over a dagger.

"Say what you came to say," she called out.

"Or are the gods only bold when the girl is cursed and alone?"

Hera laughed once, light and cruel.

Persephone's mouth twisted.

Zeus sat up straighter.

And still… Hades said nothing.

When she turned to leave, her serpents coiled tighter, heads pressed to her shoulders like shields.

The room parted.

Not from respect.

From strategy.

And Hades?

He watched her go.

No one saw the way his shadow followed after her just a little longer than it should have.

But she did.

Interlude: The God Who Didn't Kneel

She didn't hear him enter.

But she felt him.

Like gravity shifting. Like a promise unspoken.

The private chamber was dim lit only by Andreas's dying fire, now reduced to a flickering whisper in the hearth. Medusa stood with her back to the door, one hand braced on the edge of the marble basin, her reflection rippling in the dark water.

"You didn't speak," she said.

No accusation. No welcome.

Just fact.

Behind her, Hades's voice uncurled like smoke wrapped in velvet.

"Neither did you."

She turned slowly.

He was already close.

Too close.

God of shadow. King of nothing.

His eyes deep, unreadable held no judgment. Only understanding.

And that was more dangerous than anything else in Olympus.

"They'll come for you," he said.

"They already did," she replied. "And they lost."

Silence again.

He moved closer.

She didn't move back.

"You burn bright," he said. "But Olympus doesn't fear fire anymore. It uses it."

She studied him.

Not a god. Not a man.

Just… Hades.

He wasn't like the others. He never had been. And that made his silence in the court cut deeper than any blade.

"Why didn't you speak?" she asked softly.

His answer was a step closer.

Then another.

Until his hand brushed her jaw, fingers calloused and cold, but gentle.

"Because if I spoke," he said, voice low, "I might've said something I couldn't take back."

She laughed sharp, bitter.

"Like what? That you believe in me?"

"No."

A pause.

"Like the truth."

"And what's that?"

His eyes locked on hers, and for the first time, his voice trembled at the edges.

"That I want to kneel."

"But not for the court."

“Not for Olympus.”

“Only for you.”

The silence snapped.

She grabbed him by the collar and pulled him forward, lips crashing against his like war.

His hands went to her waist firm, reverent, desperate. The kiss wasn’t soft. It was all teeth and tension, the kind of kiss you gave when you didn’t know if you’d still be breathing tomorrow.

She broke away first.

Breathless. Crown askew.

“Then kneel,” she said, voice like fire stitched with venom.

He dropped to one knee.

Not as a servant.

As a man who'd made a choice.

And when her hand threaded into his hair, tilting his face upward, there was no war in her touch.

Only the promise of one to come.

Interlude: The Art of Ruin in Silk and Light

The moon hung heavy over Olympus.

Not gentle.

Not innocent.

Just... watching.

Persephone stood on the balcony of her private quarters, dark curls tangled by the wind, the scent of pomegranate and prophecy clinging to her skin. She didn't look back when the golden light behind her shifted.

Apollo had arrived.

"You're late," she said, sipping wine the colour of bloodied dusk.

"You're always waiting," he replied, stepping beside her. "Even when you're not."

He didn't touch her.

Not yet.

They didn't need to touch to scheme.

"They're watching her," Persephone said.

"Not for long," Apollo murmured. "We'll give them something better to watch."

She turned, letting her gaze sweep down his golden chest, sunlight incarnate.

Apollo was always beautiful. Always bright.

But tonight?

He was dangerous.

"And what do you suggest?" she asked, voice like shadow honey.

"Let them fall in love with a new story," he said.

"One where Medusa is a weapon, not a woman. One where Olympus is threatened, not reformed."

"And the heroes?"

He smiled.

"Us."

Persephone laughed, a sound that tasted like temptation.

Then she closed the space between them.

Her fingers dragged down his chest, slow, deliberate, calculating.

"You'd make a pretty lie, sun god."

"So would you," he breathed, cupping her waist. "A queen caught between power and danger."

"Between the underworld and the light," she whispered, lips brushing his ear.

Their mouths met in a kiss laced with secrets.

It was not love.

It was not trust.

It was strategy in silk.

Later, tangled in sheets and illusion, Apollo whispered:

"Tomorrow we plant the seed."

Persephone's lips curved against his skin.

"Let's make sure it grows into something poisonous."

Chapter One-Hundred-Sixty-Two: The First Poisoned Whisper

The Hall of Echoes was not a courtroom.

It was worse.

A place of performance, of divine memory and curated truths where what was spoken could be recorded into law by the gods who chose to believe it.And today?

Apollo and Persephone controlled the stage.

Persephone

She wore white today.

Innocent. Regal. Timeless.

The kind of white that made people forget she once wore blood beneath it.

Her hair was loose. Her voice softer than usual. And when she stood before the gathered court, she did not raise her voice.

She only whispered.

"There is no accusation," she said, hands folded. "Only... concern."

Apollo stood beside her, glowing with just enough light to look honest.

"A vision," he added, nodding solemnly. "She was not alone in the Mirror Realm."

A few gods frowned.

A few leaned closer.

"There were versions of her," Persephone said delicately. "Some dangerous. Some monstrous. One... kneeling to Zeus."

"Another crowned by vengeance," Apollo continued. "And one that destroyed the Realms."

He sighed as if the weight of his duty pained him.

"We do not say she is evil."

"We only ask" Persephone looked up, lashes low, voice trembling, "if she is whole."

The silence that followed was intentional.
And it worked.

Just enough seeds.

Just enough truth.

Just enough fear.

The recordkeeper etched it all into marble:

– A formal concern has been raised regarding the mental and magical stability of Medusa, Sovereign of the Mirror Realm.

– Investigation pending.

Persephone bowed her head.

Apollo reached for her hand, warm, theatrical, protective.

Later, in the Sunlit Gardens

"You were perfect," he whispered into her throat, lips brushing her skin like a secret.

"I always am," she replied, curling her fingers into his golden hair.

Their bodies tangled in the shade of pomegranate trees.

"Will she know it was us?" he asked between kisses.

Persephone smiled against his mouth.

"Of course."

"Good," he said.

"Let her feel it before we bring her down."

Chapter One-Hundred-Sixty-Three: The God Who Went Silent

He was late.

Andreas was never late.

Medusa stood at the edge of the scrying basin, her fingers trailing through the water, waiting for the heat of his presence to kiss her skin like it always did before he entered a room.

But the water stayed cold.

And the fire never came.

"Andreas," she whispered into the stillness.

Nothing answered.

Her serpents lifted their heads, sensing something was off. Tense. Unnatural.

She reached for him through the bond that lingered between their magic.

But all she found was smoke.

No warmth. No pain. Just... silence.

"Find him," she commanded one of her guards. "Now."

An hour passed.

Then another.

And when the owl landed on the balcony, dropping a folded note bound in silver ribbon, Medusa didn't move.

She didn't have to.

She knew.

She felt it before she even opened the letter.

Athena.

The goddess of strategy didn't scream.

She didn't stab.

She played.

The note was precise.

Elegant.

Cruel.

"Silence one flame, and the others flicker."

"Step carefully, Queen of Mirrors."

"Some crowns belong to war, not fire."

There was no name.

But the wax seal bore Athena's sigil the owl with the broken arrow.

Medusa crushed the parchment in her fist, her fingers trembling with fury.

"You want war?" she hissed.

"Then I will bring gods."

Chapter One-Hundred-Sixty-Four: The Lovers She Called to War

The court hadn't heard from her in hours.

That was their first mistake thinking silence meant surrender.

In the Temple of Storm glass, under the glow of realm fire and wrath, Medusa stood like a prophecy made flesh. Her gown was gone. She wore leather and war-silk. Her serpents were coiled into braids down her spine, each one hissing like it could taste the coming blood.

And then the doors opened.

Three gods entered.

Each one had once kissed her.

Each one still would burn Olympus if she asked.

Hercules arrived first.

"I heard Andreas's missing," he said. His jaw was set. His fists, bare. "You don't call me unless we're breaking things."

"We are," she said. "And then we're bringing him home."

Ares came second.

He didn't ask.

He just tossed a blade at her feet a sword once dipped in hydra venom and phoenix ash.

"Let's bleed someone," he growled.

Hades appeared last.

Silent. Still.

But when their eyes met, there was no hesitation. No apology for leaving. No explanation.

Just a nod.

"Say the word," he said.

She did not smile.

She only spoke:

"Athena took him. She thinks it will make me kneel."

She stepped forward, picking up Ares's blade.

"We ride at dusk."

They suited up in silence.

Ares laced her armour.

Hercules saddled the beasts.

Hades brought the map etched in obsidian, marked in salt and shadow, where Athena's forces were hiding Andreas.

"Are you sure?" Hades asked once, low. "If you go... Olympus will spin it. They'll make you the villain."

Medusa looked up, crownless but not uncrowned.

"Then let them."

"Let them fear me."

"Let them see what happens when you touch what's mine."

As they rode into the storm, three gods at her back and war in her bones...

Medusa didn't look back.

She was the storm now.

Chapter One-Hundred-Sixty-Five: The Day Olympus Forgot Her Name

The throne room was not empty.

It was waiting.

Athena stepped across the marble floor with the precision of a goddess who never asked for power only planned for the moment everyone else lost it.

Behind her, Persephone walked in silence, lips painted the shade of pomegranate lies.

Beside her, Apollo glowed like morning after a funeral.

The court hadn't summoned them.

But they came anyway.

"The Mirror Queen has left Olympus," Athena said to the assembled gods. "Unannounced. With three gods at her back. In pursuit of personal vengeance."

Gasps rippled through the chamber.

"She took Ares. She took Hades. She took Hercules," Apollo added, voice solemn. "She left Olympus unguarded."

"She left it unruled," Athena said.

Zeus did not speak.

He had left days ago retreating to the edge of the heavens to "contemplate balance."

Coward.

Hera watched, lips tight. But she did not rise.

No one did.

Because the gods knew what Athena always had:

Power isn't taken. It's abandoned.

Athena reached the base of the throne.

Not Medusa's mirror dais.

The true throne.

Olympus itself.

And she did not ask.

She did not kneel.

She only turned to the court and spoke:

"As Regent of Order and Guardian of Divine Stability, I hereby assume temporary control of Olympus until a full council review."

"Let the records show: Medusa is absent."

"And Olympus does not serve absence."

A clerk stepped forward with the marble record scroll.

Apollo smiled as he spoke the final word:

"Motion carried."

The recordkeeper etched the words into stone:

– The Mirror Sovereign is to be reviewed upon return.

– Interim authority: Athena.

Persephone stepped closer to Athena as the seal was stamped.

"Do you think she'll come back?" she whispered.

Athena's eyes didn't blink.

"Yes."

"And when she does…"

She turned, expression unreadable.

"She'll find her name already erased."

Chapter One-Hundred-Sixty-Six: The Path of Wings and Fire

The cliffs narrowed.

What began as a war march now felt like a trap.

Stone walls rose on either side jagged, high, perfect for ambush. Wind howled above the canyon, sharp and shrill, but Medusa didn't flinch. She trusted her serpents to hear what her ears couldn't.

They hissed once.

Then the sky screamed.

Harpies descended like winged knives.

Six. No eight. Clawed limbs, rancid feathers, teeth like broken glass. They didn't speak. They shrieked.

Hercules was already in front of her.

He moved like rage, bare arms catching the first harpy mid-lunge, slamming it into stone.

"You, okay?" he barked, voice rough.

Medusa didn't answer.

Another harpy dove. She ducked, rolled, slashed upward with a blade of celestial bone.

"Fine," she growled, rising in a whirl of serpents and silk. "Next time, don't block the view."

Hercules grinned.

"You like the view?"

"I like my kill count higher than yours."

Ares was laughing now two harpies impaled on his spear, blood glinting like rubies. He was soaked in sweat and sin, a war god drunk on carnage.

"Are these Athena's pets?" he shouted.

"Too stupid for hers," Hades muttered from behind a shadow-wrought shield.

Then Medusa saw it.

One harpy the largest landed on a ledge just above her. Its wings flared. Across the inner joint of its left wing, something glowed.

A sigil.

Burned into its flesh.

Athena's crest.

Her blood went cold.

"This wasn't a chance attack," she breathed.

Hercules stood beside her, panting.

"You sure?"

She reached up and sliced the sigil from the harpy's still-smoking corpse.

"I'm certain."

After the battle, the canyon smelled of blood and smoke.

They camped just beyond the ridge, wind drying their wounds. Ares stripped off his armour first, throwing it in a pile.

"She's testing us," he muttered, lying back on the stone. "Wants to see if we're still dangerous."

"She should've remembered," Medusa said softly, "we always were."

That night, Hercules sat beside her.

No armour. No jokes. Just quiet.

You know I'd follow you into Tartarus, right?"

She looked at him. The fire danced in his eyes, same heat, same ache.

"I never asked you to."

"You didn't have to."

Their lips almost touched.

Almost.

But Medusa turned away.

"Andreas comes first."

He nodded. But the hunger didn't fade.

Neither did hers.

Chapter One-Hundred-Sixty-Seven: The Eye That Watched Them Burn

The gorge looked like it had been carved by flame.

Black stone. Boiling mist. A bridge of broken obsidian stretched across the chasm wide enough for one. Maybe.

"This is a trap," Ares muttered.

Hades didn't respond. He stood beside Medusa, shadows swirling at his boots.

"You say that like it matters," Medusa said.

"It matters if we die," Hercules offered from behind, flexing a shoulder that still bled from a harpy's talon.

"Then don't die," Ares snapped.

They started across.

One by one.

Medusa in the lead, her serpents tasting the air.
Then Hades silent, unreadable. Hercules next.
Ares last.

Halfway across, the stone shuddered.

And from the mist below

A roar.

Not echo. Not wind.

Something waking.

Something huge.

The Cyclops rose from the pit like a mountain given breath.

One eye. Burning. A forge of hatred.

His skin was cracked obsidian, molten veins pulsing with heat. A hammer the size of a tree slung over his back.

He roared again and leapt onto the bridge.

Ares ran forward.

"Finally," he whispered, eyes lighting with warlust.

"We need to get across!" Hades called.

"We need him dead!" Ares shouted back.

He met the Cyclops mid-span, blade against hammer. The sound shook the gorge.

Behind him, Medusa sprinted, Hades beside her. Hercules turned, watching Ares with a tension that wasn't just concern it was recognition.

"He's doing it again," Hercules growled. "Proving something, no one asked him to."

Medusa didn't turn back.

"Then let him."

The Cyclops slammed Ares into the bridge. A crack split beneath them.

But Ares laughed bloodied, grinning.

"I've fought Titans with better aim."

He lunged, sliced, dodged heat swirling off his skin.

"Come on, you one-eyed bastard," he taunted.
Give me a reason to scream your name!"

Medusa's voice cut through the steam.

"You always scream names in battle?"

"Only when it's hot!"

They made it across.

Just as Ares drove his blade through the
Cyclops' eye, letting it fall burning into the pit.

He staggered to the far side, panting, shirtless,
arms streaked with soot and blood.

"Well?" he said, tossing his blade down beside
Medusa's feet. "Still think I'm reckless?"

She didn't answer.

She just looked at him long, slow, the way one
watches a storm gather on the horizon.

"I think you're burning for the wrong reason," she said.

That night, Ares didn't speak.

But he sat beside her fire.

Close enough to touch.

And far enough that it hurt.

Chapter One-Hundred-Sixty-Eight: The Sky Cracks with His Name

The air changed after sundown.

Not colder. Not calmer.

Heavier.

They made camp beneath the twisted roots of an ancient, petrified tree. Its bark gleamed silver under the starlight, fossilized in a shape that looked like something had screamed through it once.

Hades stood watch back straight, face quiet, cloak like smoke coiling around him.

Medusa didn't sleep.

Neither did the sky.

The first crack of thunder wasn't sound.

It was pressure.

The fire went out on its own.

Wind howled, branches bent, and lightning flared purple across the clouds.

"That's no storm," Hercules said, stepping from the shadows.

"Typhon," Hades whispered, his eyes glowing dimly.

"You're sure?" Medusa asked.

"I would know the smell of him anywhere," Hades murmured. "He was caged under Tartarus. If he walks, someone opened the gate."

The wind roared.

And Typhon descended.

He didn't land.

He fell.

A streak of monstrous wings and storm light,
colliding with the ground in a quake of fury.
Heads like snakes writhed from his shoulders.
His body was smoke, lightning, scaled shadow.

And his voice

"Queen of Venom. Child of Ruin. Turn back."

Medusa didn't flinch.

"You speak in riddles, monster," she growled.

"I speak for Athena."

"Then die for her."

They fought beneath a sky split with fire.

Typhon moved like a hurricane in the shape of a god. Hercules took the first hit, launched backwards into stone. Ares charged next, only to be thrown with a scream.

Medusa dodged.

Then

Hades caught her.

His shadows surged around her like armour.

He dragged her beneath the old-world tree, shielding her from a crack of divine lightning.

"Stay still," he ordered, voice low.

"You're shaking," she whispered.

He looked at her.

"Not from fear."

The lightning flared again.

And for one fragile moment beneath that silver-barked canopy, wind howling like prophecy she reached for him.

He met her halfway.

Not lips.

But foreheads, pressed together, heat and shadow merging.

"We were never made for peace," she whispered.

"No," Hades said, his breath like smoke. "But gods like us were born to burn."

Together, they rose.

Together, they fought.

And when Typhon finally fell writhing,

shattered they didn't speak of what passed

beneath that tree.

But they remembered.

Chapter One-Hundred-Sixty-Nine: Labyrinth of Fire and Teeth

The forest broke open into a crater of stone.

Twisted pillars rose like ribs from the earth marking the entrance to something older than Olympus, older than the gods who ruled it.

The Labyrinth.

"This isn't just a ruin," Medusa murmured.

"It's a warning," Hercules said.

"It's a trap," Ares added, already smiling.

They entered at dusk.

Flames flickered from torches that no one had lit. The air was thick not with heat, but breath.

The ground trembled before they saw him.

The Minotaur.

Towering. Fur scorched with ancient burns. Horns etched with blood-runes that glowed faintly in the dark. His axe scraped the stone as he walked.

Behind him...

The Chimera.

A lion's head roared fire. A serpent tail hissed. The goat's head, silent, watched them with dead eyes.

"Athena," Medusa said, voice tight.

"No doubt," Hercules growled.

They didn't speak after that.

Only fought.

Hercules lunged for the Minotaur, matching brute force with brute fury.

Ares faced the Chimera, laughing even as its tail coiled around his leg and flung him against a wall.

Medusa moved like prophecy fast, furious, lethal.

Her blade caught the Chimera's lion mouth just as it flared to breathe. She twisted. The fire shot sideways lighting the maze.

"It's alive," she gasped.

The walls shifted.

Stone moved.

The Minotaur bellowed in rage.

And somewhere in the smoke

Pegasus screamed.

A crash.

A crack of hooves.

Centaurs charged from the flame, wielding radiant bows and blades carved of starlight. They surrounded the Chimera, pushing it back.

From above, Pegasus descended, his white wings scorched, eyes wild.

"He found us," Medusa whispered.

"He was sent," Hades corrected, stepping from the shadow of the moving walls. "The Labyrinth serves power. You've reminded it who you are."

The Minotaur fell to Hercules' final blow.

The Chimera screamed as the centaurs pierced its hearts.

The fire died with it.

Pegasus landed.

A centaur approached his mane silver, his eyes ancient.

"Come. There is no time. The boy you seek is beyond the Vale of Glass. We will guide you."

"Andreas," Medusa breathed.

Her fists clenched.

Her serpents rose.

"Hold on," Ares said, brushing dust from his chest. "Didn't we just nearly die?"

"Yes," Medusa said. "And now we do it again."

Chapter One-Hundred-Seventy: The Vale of Glass

They followed the centaurs into the valley of mirrors.

Not literal ones.

But every surface reflected.

The ground glimmered like crystal. The sky shimmered with fractured light. Even the trees twisted, metallic things glinted with reflections that weren't quite real.

"This is dangerous," Hades said, drawing close.

"It's beautiful," Hercules whispered.

"It's a lie," Ares growled.

The centaur leader turned.

"This place does not kill with weapons. It kills with memory."

"Whose?" Medusa asked.

"Yours."

They walked in silence.

And that's when it began.

A flicker in the glass beside her.

Andreas.

Not wounded. Not afraid.

Smiling.

"You left me," the vision whispered.

Medusa froze.

It wasn't real.

And yet her heart slammed into her ribs.

"Andreas?" she whispered.

"You chose gods," the reflection said, "and left me in the dark."

"He's not real," Hades said, voice sharp.

"No," Ares added. "But your guilt is."

They kept walking.

More visions appeared.

Hercules saw a battlefield. His brothers, bleeding. His father turning away.

Ares saw blood on his hands not enemies, but lovers. Gods. A boy with eyes like shame.

Hades saw a crown.

And a throne.

And her Persephone walking away.

"This place isn't just memory," Medusa murmured. "It's a mirror of regret."

She clenched her fists.

"I won't be ruled by what I didn't do."

The serpent at her shoulder hissed, and her eyes flared.

She shattered the mirror with a scream.

Glass rained like stars.

The reflections screamed with it.

And through the storm

She heard Andreas's real voice.

Not from a mirror.

From the mountain.

"Help me!"

She turned.

Ran.

And the centaur leader called after her

"Only the truth can survive the Vale."

Chapter One-Hundred-Seventy-One: Where the Boy Waited (And the Gods Bled to Find Him)

They reached the mountain's throat by dawn.

Clawed paths twisted through obsidian and ice. The centaurs stayed behind. Pegasus flew overhead, circling, restless.

Medusa led the way.

Each step forward stole her breath, not from effort but from knowing.

Andreas was close.

"This place was built for punishment," Hades muttered, eyes scanning the jagged stone. "Not prison."

"There's no difference in Olympus," Ares growled.

"No," Hercules added, "but the difference is who they punish."

The entrance was carved with runes Medusa had never seen.

They pulsed when she passed.

Inside, the air turned warm too warm. Metallic.

Like blood just spilled.

She didn't hesitate.

Andreas was chained.

Arms above his head. Shirt torn. Cuts across his chest. But his eyes

Alive.

"You came," he breathed.

"Of course I did," Medusa whispered, kneeling beside him.

"You shouldn't have."

"Why?"

"Because she's not done yet."

The shadows moved.

And Athena's voice filled the room.

"Touch him again, and I'll slit his soul down the middle."

Hades stepped forward.

"You dare?"

"I warned you not to bring her to Olympus," Athena hissed.

"You stole him from me," Medusa said, rising slowly. "Because you knew you couldn't erase me."

"Not erase," Athena said, stepping from the dark. "Replace."

She wore a crown now.

A new one.

Forged in silver and public favour.

"They want a queen who doesn't fall for monsters," Athena said, voice like a knife. "I'm giving them one."

Behind her, Apollo stepped into the light.

"You all played your part well," he said smoothly. "Tragedy. Lust. War. Perfect for a cautionary tale."

"And now?" Ares asked.

"Now, we give the world a resurrection," Apollo said.

"You made me a villain," Medusa said.

"You made yourself interesting," Athena countered. "We just added the ending."

Medusa reached for her blade.

Hercules reached for his axe.

Hades was already moving.

But then

Andreas screamed.

The chain flared with light.

Divine blood magic.

"They anchored it to her," Hades growled. "To Medusa."

And just like that, they were trapped.

Because if Medusa moved to strike

Andreas would die.

Chapter One-Hundred-Seventy-Two: The Gods Who Took the Fall

Andreas's scream was still echoing when the magic surged.

It wasn't just pain it was punishment. Divine, precise, personal.

Hades froze mid-strike.

Hercules dropped his axe.

Even Ares hesitated.

"He's tethered to you," Hades said. "Any violent act from you... and the pain echoes through his blood."

"Athena bound him with intent," Hercules added. "Blood for blood. Bond for bond."

"Then let's give her something worse than violence," Medusa whispered, stepping forward.

Apollo raised a brow.

"What could be worse than that?"

"Being forgotten," Medusa said. "Losing the story."

Her eyes met the shadows. Not Athena. Not Apollo.

The people.

The unseen gods.

The realm itself.

"They want a villain," she said louder now, voice rising. "They want a queen they can burn."

She knelt beside Andreas.

Softly.

Not defeated.

Deciding.

"Then let's give them the gods who bled to keep their thrones."

She looked at Hades.

Then Hercules.

Then Ares.

"Drop your weapons."

"What?" Ares growled.

"Let Olympus see who starts the war."

One by one, they obeyed.

And with every blade that clanged to the floor

The chain around Andreas weakened.

Not by force.

By narrative.

Athena stepped back.

"You're trying to out-myth me?"
"No," Medusa said, standing over Andreas.
"I'm reminding them who made the myths to
begin with."

A flare of golden light burst through the
chamber not from a god.

From the Vale of Glass.

Reflections surged.

Witnesses arrived.

Mirrors hovering in mid-air. Portals of memory. Truths no longer hidden.

"They're watching," Hades said, low and dangerous.

"They've always been watching," Medusa replied.

And with the entire realm bearing witness

Andreas's chains shattered.

Athena screamed.

Apollo vanished.

The mountain shook with the sound of truth unchained.

Chapter One-Hundred-Seventy-Three: The Throne They Couldn't Burn

The mountain was still smoking when they returned to Olympus.

Andreas was half-carried by Hercules, wrapped in one of Hades' cloaks. His wounds glowed faintly, marked with runes that had begun to fade the moment Medusa shattered the myth.

And Olympus?

Olympus had changed.

They walked through gates that no longer shimmered with Athena's favour.

The crowd parted.

The sky pulsed.

The realm itself had begun to rewrite.

"They expected to see me chained," Medusa murmured.

"They expected to see you broken," Hades corrected.

"But instead," Andreas whispered, voice raw, "they're seeing the queen who wouldn't burn."

The throne room doors opened.

Empty.

Except for the seat of power still warm from betrayal.

Medusa didn't sit.

Not yet.

She looked at the gods who stood before her now: bruised, defiant, loyal.

Ares, arms crossed, jaw clenched.
Hercules, hands at his sides, gaze protective.
Hades, in the shadows, but never once turning away.

Andreas, watching her like she was prophecy incarnate.

And then she turned to the crowd gathering in the reflection pool where the Realm itself watched.

"I am not here to take a throne," Medusa said, voice ringing like storm light. "I am here to change it."

The serpents at her crown hissed once, and curled like a coronation.

"This throne has burned queens before. It will not burn me."

She stepped forward.

And this time

She sat.

And Olympus, for the first time in centuries, bowed.

Chapter One-Hundred-Seventy-Four: The Goddess Who Wrote Her Own Ending

The throne didn't burn her.

It bent.

Curved beneath the weight of something it had never carried before a queen who didn't need its favour to rule.

Medusa sat, spine straight, gaze level.

Her crown of serpents shimmered with restrained fury. Her dress, spun from starlight and prophecy, moved like memory.

And before her, Olympus held its breath.

"This realm has broken queens," she said softly. "Twisted them into monsters. Painted them as warnings."

She rose slowly, her voice growing stronger with each step down the marble dais.
"I am not a warning."

"I am what comes after."

Ares looked like he might fall to his knees again but not from defeat.

From devotion.

Hercules stood with arms crossed, jaw tense, hiding the ache of desire and the fear of what comes next.

Hades watched from the shadows, silent. But his eyes burned with something Medusa could no longer name love sharpened by inevitability.

Andreas, still recovering, leaned against a column with runes faintly glowing on his skin. But his eyes never left her. Not once.

The silence cracked.

And Olympus began to move again.

Not with applause.

With whispers.

"She won't last."

"The gods will never follow her."

"Where is Athena? Who speaks for the old laws?"

Medusa let them speak.

Then she lifted her hand, and the mirrors answered.

Dozens of glass portals shimmered into being, hovering above the crowd.

Each one pulsed with visions of her past. Her sacrifice. Her rise. Her fire.

"You've seen who I was," she said. "Now watch what I become."

One by one, gods stepped forward.

Some to bow.

Some to threaten.

But all to bear witness.

The era of burnt queens had ended.

The era of self-written endings had begun.

Behind her, the throne whispered temptations.

Ahead of her, Olympus bristled with unrest.

And within her power still rising.

Chapter One-Hundred-Seventy-Five: The Game of Crowns

The throne may have accepted her.

But Olympus had not.

It was clear in the way the gods gathered not in reverence, but in ritual. A test. A performance. Each one waiting for her to trip over old laws and newer grudges.

Medusa stood at the centre of the hall, the crown of serpents gleaming, her chin high.

They called it a court.

But it was war dressed in robes and riddles.

"They want a queen," Hades whispered behind her, "but only if they can claim her."

"Then let them try," she murmured, "and watch how they burn."

The Performance of the Gods

Dionysus arrived first drunk on power and perfume, his words slurred but sharp.

"You'll need a festival, my dear. A coronation soaked in wine and spectacle. Otherwise, they'll forget you before the ambrosia cools."

He kissed her hand.

She didn't flinch.

Hermes circled next, sly as smoke.

"A little chaos might help," he mused. "Turn the whispers to rumours. Make them afraid to speak your name at all."

Demeter stayed silent. But the vines curling at her feet told Medusa enough.

Poseidon didn't come.

He'd sent a wave instead. A subtle threat. The ocean would rise or retreat depending on her choices.

And then came Ares his armour gleaming, lips pursed in quiet fury.

"You shouldn't have let them see you bleed," he said. "Power must be worshipped. Not wept over."

"You worship me just fine," Medusa said, stepping close. "And I bleed better than you burn."

His eyes flared.

His hands curled.

And he stepped back.

Not in fear.

In restraint.

Because if he touched her here he would not stop.

"The court sees everything," Hades reminded her later that night.

"Then let them see this," she replied, throwing open the doors to her war chamber.

The game had begun.

And queens?

They didn't play.

They rewrote.

Chapter One-Hundred-Seventy-Six: The Gods Who Whisper in Shadows

Apollo's POV Schemes, Silk, and Poisoned Promises

They didn't see him.

Not properly.

Apollo knew how to shine when the stage demanded it but in moments like this, he preferred the dark. The hush before thunder. The breath held before a scream.

He moved through Olympus' back halls, golden robes abandoned for something simpler. Cloaked. Discreet.

Because now wasn't the time for sunlight.

Now was the time for whispers.

"She's weakening them," Persephone said, appearing beside him in the corridor like a rose blooming where no root should grow. "One kiss at a time."

"They're not gods anymore," Apollo muttered. "They're men chasing heat."

"And she?" Persephone asked.

"She's the fire."

They paused at a mirror.

Not just any mirror.

One of Athena's old conduits a silent watcher. Still alive with residual power.

Apollo ran his finger along the frame.

"She has the throne," he said. "But she doesn't know what it costs."

"We'll show her," Persephone murmured.

"No," Apollo corrected. "We'll make Olympus show her."

They stepped through shadowed hallways, making soft promises to powerful ears.

To the Fates, he offered silence if they stayed blind a little longer.

To Hestia, he offered peace in exchange for inaction.

To the minor gods, he offered elevation titles, shrines, a return to reverence.

It wasn't war yet.

But it would be.

And when it was, no one would remember Medusa as a queen.

Only as a scandal.

A lover.

A mistake.

"She thinks they love her," Persephone whispered as they watched Hades step into Medusa's chamber later that night.

"She's not wrong," Apollo replied, smiling.

"And that's why we'll win."

Interlude: The Fire They Pretended Not to Feel

Persephone didn't blink as the chamber door closed behind Hades.

The soft sound echoed in her ears like a verdict.

"She thinks they love her," she had whispered. And now, that whisper wouldn't stop echoing in her own chest.

"She's not wrong," Apollo had said, with that maddening smile.

But as they stood in the hidden corridor, watching the shadows flicker, something else burned brighter than jealousy.

Desire.

Not for Hades. Not for Medusa.

But for control.

"She's not the only one who knows how to command a room," Persephone murmured, stepping closer to Apollo.

He arched a golden brow, amused, but his stance didn't shift.

Not yet.

"You want to prove something?" he asked.

"No," she said, unfastening the clasp at her throat. "I want to remind you who taught Olympus how to beg."

The silk fell in a whisper.

Apollo inhaled sharply.

His resolve shattered in a blink.

Their kiss was not gentle.

It was punishment.

Lust sharpened by resentment. Worship laced with venom.

She pushed him back against the mirror, and it groaned bearing witness as her fingers slid under his robe, as his hands clutched her hips like a prayer he couldn't finish.

"You think she's fire?" Persephone said between gasps. "Watch what ice does when it melts."

Apollo gripped her tighter. "Then melt for me."

They didn't care who saw.

Let Olympus watch.

Let the gods pretend they didn't wish they were
the ones burning like this.

Because in that moment, under the jealous
moon and the weight of unspoken truths, they
weren't planning Medusa's downfall.

They were proving they still knew how to take.

And be taken.

Chapter One-Hundred-Seventy-Seven: The Lovers Who Knew Better

Ares heard the lie first.

Not from Medusa's lips, but in the silence that followed her touch.

She had told them she was fine.

That Olympus would fall in line.

That love was enough to hold the throne.

But gods forged in blood knew better than to trust silence.

"She's unravelling," Ares muttered, pacing the edges of the war chamber like a caged beast. "Not outwardly. Not yet. But it's there."

"You want her to admit it?" Hercules asked, arms crossed, jaw clenched. "Would you?"

"No," Ares said. "I'd burn first."

They stood together, but it didn't feel like unity.

It felt like mourning.

For something they hadn't lost yet but could.

Hercules stepped forward, pulling a scroll from behind his belt.

"This came through the lower rings. Minor gods whispering of deals. Old allegiances shifting."

"Apollo?" Ares guessed.

"And Persephone. Maybe Athena."

The name alone was enough to make Ares still.

"That witch doesn't play games," he said. "She makes rules."

"And she's making new ones," Hercules growled.

They didn't speak for a moment.

Didn't need to.

Because both knew what came next.

They would need to protect her.

Even if it meant fighting the gods they once stood beside.

"She'll never ask for help," Ares said finally.

"Good," Hercules replied, cracking his knuckles. "I prefer to offer it with a sword."

Behind them, the doors to the chamber opened.

And Medusa stepped in, fierce, regal, and burning.

But Ares saw it, the flicker in her gaze.

The weight.

And he realized then...

She didn't need their help.

She needed their faith.

Chapter One-Hundred-Seventy-Eight: The Whisper War Begins

The rumours came like smoke.

Not loud. Not sharp. Just... curling around everything she touched.

They whispered in corners, flitted through chambers, bled into scrolls and side-eyes.

And Medusa Queen of Olympus, crowned in fire and defiance was suddenly a woman with too many lovers and not enough control.

"They're calling me a whore with a crown," she said, voice like ice under pressure.

"You're a goddess," Hecate answered from the shadows. "They always call us that, right before they kneel."

Still, Medusa couldn't ignore it.

Not because she cared what they said.

But because it was working.

The minor gods were withdrawing.

The elders hesitated.

And somewhere deep in the political rot of Olympus...

Athena was smiling.

Andreas was still gone.

His absence was a bruise she didn't speak of, but it throbbed with every hour. And it told her one truth louder than any rumour:

This isn't war. Not yet. But it will be.

"Start listening," she told the mirrors. "To the lies. To the truths they're hiding."

The glass pulsed. Obeyed.

And within its flickering surface, Medusa saw it

- Apollo kissing a senator's hand.
- Persephone whispering in a priestess's ear.
- Athena sitting on the Council steps.

Not speaking.

Just being seen.

"They're rewriting me," she said aloud.

"Then write louder," said Hecate, handing her a dagger made of onyx and oath.

That night, Medusa stood alone on the balcony of Olympus and made a vow.

Not with rage.

With clarity.

"You can whisper all you like," she murmured to the stars.

"I will answer with thunder."

Interlude: The Balcony Where Gods Burned Softly

The night was thick with silence.

Not peace. Not rest.

But the kind of silence that came before kingdoms cracked.

Medusa didn't turn when he stepped onto the balcony.

She didn't have to.

"They're whispering again," Hercules said.

"Let them whisper," she replied. "It won't save them."

But her hands trembled on the marble rail.

Just once.

And Hercules saw it.

He crossed the space between them in two steps.

Not with command.

With gravity.

"You're allowed to break," he said, his voice rough with something older than war. "Just not alone."

She didn't answer. But when he brushed her hair aside and placed his lips at the back of her neck, she didn't stop him either.

The first kiss wasn't lust.

It was relief.

The second?

Need.

By the third, she was arching into him like the stars could bear witness.

"You still want me?" she asked, voice sharp with challenge and soft with fear.

"Every night. Every war. Every version of you they've tried to erase."

He turned her around.

Lifted her onto the stone ledge as if she weighed nothing.

Not a queen.

Not a goddess.

Just her.

His mouth moved like worship across her collarbone.

His hands, reverent and rough, found the parts of her no one else had touched not recently. Not right.

"They'll see," she whispered.

"Let them," he growled against her skin. "Let them know you're not theirs."

And when she wrapped her legs around his waist and pulled him closer

Olympus held its breath.

Because power wasn't just won in war rooms.

Sometimes, it was forged in the dark.

With sweat.

With surrender.

With the kind of intimacy only gods brave enough to feel could survive.

Chapter One-Hundred-Seventy-Nine: The Dagger Behind the Smile

Persephone smiled sweetly as she poured wine into the council chalice.

A soft tilt of her wrist.

A whisper of roses and venom.

Across from her, the Oracle didn't blink.

"These vintage tastes... unusual," the Oracle said.

"Truth often does," Persephone replied.

The Council table had once been Olympus's pride.

Now, it was its most dangerous battleground.

No swords. No armies.

Just glances, rumours, and perfectly timed pauses.

Apollo leaned back in his chair, watching her with amused detachment.

To the others, they looked like allies.

To the wise?

Co-conspirators.

"Medusa grows popular," said Dionysus, running a finger along the stem of his goblet. "The people love her fire."

"They always love a flame," Persephone murmured, "until it burns down their temples."

The room laughed politely.

But the Oracle's gaze sharpened.

Persephone knew the dance.

Charm.

Defer.

Strike.

She wasn't Athena blunt and brutal.

She was silk stretched over a blade.

And she knew exactly how to cut without bleeding.

"Let us speak plainly," she said, standing. "The Queen grows reckless. Her power stretches too far, too fast. Olympus needs balance. It needs... clarity."

"It needs control," Apollo added lazily.

"It needs us," Persephone finished.

Silence followed.

Then nods.

Small. Measured. Dangerous.

As the council recessed, Persephone leaned
into Apollo's ear.

"By the time she realizes what we've done," she
whispered, "she'll be fighting shadows."

"And losing worship," he replied, "faster than
her lovers can please her."

They smiled.

And beneath the marble floor, Olympus
shivered.

Chapter One-Hundred-Eighty: The Throne That Would Not Bend

They thought they could shame her into silence.

Thought whispers could unseat a woman who had risen from ashes with gods at her feet and crowns in her fists.

But thrones made of prophecy and vengeance do not bend.

They burn.

Medusa walked into the Hall of Pillars alone.

No guards.

No lovers.

No crown.

Just herself and the promise of ruin stitched into her spine.

The room fell silent.

Even the walls listened.

"You've all been very loud," she said, her voice silk-wrapped steel.

"So, allow me to speak clearly."

She climbed the dais like it owed her an apology.

Turned to face the council.

And sat on the throne as if it had never belonged to anyone else.

"I was not made to be liked," she continued.

"I was made to rule."

"With chaos?" one of the senators dared to ask.

"With truth," she said. "And if the truth makes you tremble, perhaps you should not be standing where gods reside."

She felt them Apollo, Persephone, even Athena watching her through veils of calculation.

But none of them moved.

Because deep down, they all remembered:

She didn't take Olympus with armies.

She took it by surviving what none of them could.

Her voice dropped to a whisper that still reached every corner.

"Say what you like. Spread your lies. But know this"

"I will not bend.

I will not break.

And when I burn, I burn through."

The throne pulsed beneath her like it agreed.

And as Medusa looked down on a room full of cowards in silk and power-hungry traitors

She smiled.

"Now," she said, voice colder than prophecy. "Kneel."

Chapter One-Hundred-Eighty-One: A Doubt Between Gods

The stars were hidden tonight.

Not by clouds.

By choice.

Apollo didn't trust even the moonlight anymore.

He arrived first, of course.

He always did.

And when Persephone slipped into the forgotten temple, her cloak of midnight petals trailing behind her, he didn't smile.

Not this time.

"We're being watched," she said.

"We're always being watched," he replied, voice like golden dusk. "We built Olympus on mirrors and whispers."

She came to stand beside him, hands folded.

Close.

But not touching.

Not tonight.

"You hesitate," she said after a while.

"No," he answered too quickly. "I calculate."

Persephone turned to face him fully.

Eyes no longer soft with spring.

Hard now. Frosted. Regal.

"You were always the one who believed in truth. In light."

"And you were always the one who said truth is a luxury," he countered. "We gave them a goddess who burns. We must be the ones who endure."

He stepped closer.

Just enough.

"But do you ever wonder," he whispered, "what it would be like... to follow her instead?"

Persephone's expression didn't change.

But her breath caught.

"You forget your place."

"No," he said. "I remember hers."

The silence between them ached.

And something fragile dangerous stirred in its folds.

"If you waver," she said, stepping back, "don't expect me to follow."

"I never do," he replied.

But as she left, the night colder in her absence

Apollo did not move.

Because for the first time since the plot began...

He wasn't sure they were right.

Chapter One-Hundred-Eighty-Two: The Queen Who Played the Long Game

They had underestimated her.

Again.

Let them.

Let them believe she was driven by emotion, not strategy.

Let them mistake silence for surrender.

Because while they whispered and schemed...

Medusa moved.

In the deepest chamber of the palace, a place even gods had forgotten, she unrolled a scroll marked not with ink but with blood and binding.

Andreas had found it, once.

Old magic. Forbidden. Almost sentient.

Now?

It would serve her.

"Bring them," she told the priestess. "The ones no one remembers."

And so they came.

One by one.

Not nobles. Not generals.

But those who had nothing left to lose and everything to burn.

Former Titans.

Exiled gods.

The quiet, the broken, the too-powerful-to-be-trusted.

Medusa welcomed them all.

"Olympus doesn't need another war," she said.

"It needs a reminder of what happens when queens are provoked."

By morning, three minor temples burned.

No one was hurt.

But the message was clear:

She knew.

And she wasn't afraid to start playing their game, better.

When Hades, Ares, and Hercules found her
that night, her hair still smelled of smoke.

"You started a war," Hades said quietly.

"No," she corrected. "I reminded them who
they're trying to dethrone."

And when Andreas returned dragged from
shadow by the same network Medusa had
revived in silence he didn't ask how.

He just knelt.

"You never stopped planning," he whispered.

She touched his chin, raised his gaze.

"I never stopped remembering."

Because queens didn't always scream when
they were betrayed.

Sometimes?

They played the long game.

And checkmate came with a crown.

Interlude: The Heat Between Words

The map room was empty.

Except for them.

And the war they were pretending not to fight.

Not the war of Olympus.

The one between glances. Between breaths.

Medusa leaned over the table, fingers brushing the parchment.

Her voice low. Measured.

"If we move here, we'll cut off Athena's eastern supply route. She won't expect it."

Behind her, Hercules stepped closer.

Not for the map.

For her.

"You're not sleeping again," he said softly.

"Because I'm planning," she replied, not turning.

"You're burning," he corrected.

His breath ghosted the back of her neck.

And still, she didn't turn.

Not yet.

"Tell me to stop," he said, voice a velvet knife.

"I never do."

She turned.

Slowly.

And the space between them didn't survive it.

Their lips didn't crash. They hovered millimetres of agony, restraint

A promise unclaimed.

"Not here," she whispered.

"Why not?" he breathed.

"Because if I start..." Her hand slid up his chest. "I won't stop."

And neither would he.

But the war her war still burned brighter than either of them.

So instead...

They parted.

Barely.

And the map remained untouched.

But the fire?

It grew.

Chapter One-Hundred-Eighty-Three: Apollo at the Crossroads

There were no hymns in this temple anymore.

Only dust.

And doubt.

Apollo stood beneath the ruined archway where once, offerings had spilled like wine, where light had been his weapon, his glory, his truth.

But now?

He wasn't sure what truth even meant anymore.

"She doesn't deserve the crown," he whispered to no one.

"But gods help me, she wears it better than the rest of us ever did."

The words felt like betrayal.

Because they were.

Persephone's voice still echoed in his mind from nights past.

"If you waver…"

He had.

He was.

And as the golden god of prophecy stared into the future, he saw only a battlefield…

With Medusa at the centre.

Crowned in fire.

Eyes like judgment.

And beside her

not him.

"You were meant to bring balance," he told

himself. "Not chaos."

But even he didn't believe it anymore.

Because what the gods called chaos

Medusa called justice.

And maybe, just maybe…

she was right.

Interlude: The Scroll That Shouldn't be Answered.

The scroll arrived wrapped in white silk.

No seal.

No name.

Just light perfume, barely clinging to the fabric
honeysuckle and blood orange.

Medusa.

Apollo didn't open it right away.

He stood at the edge of the sun temple's ruins,
scroll in hand, wondering how far was too far
to fall.

He was already cracking.

This might break him.

But curiosity?

That had always been his godhood's flaw.

He unrolled it.

One line.

"We both know Olympus is a performance.
Shall we begin the second act together?"

No threats.

No commands.

Not even a signature.

But he heard her voice in it low, certain,
seductive with intent and power.

He should have burned it.

He should have taken it to Athena.

He should have

"Damn you," he whispered.

"And damn me for admiring the way you play."

By nightfall, he was at the edge of her territory.

He didn't ask for permission.

He waited.

And when the wind shifted, carrying
honeysuckle once more, the air shimmered

And she stepped into view.

Medusa.

Wearing nothing but war-readiness and the
smile of someone who knew the end was near.

"You came," she said, voice unreadable.

"To warn you," he lied.

"To watch me," she corrected.

And they both knew...

Something irreversible had begun.

Interlude: Beneath the Silk of Strategy

The chamber was not a bedroom.

It was a war room draped in velvet, built for whispers, not surrender.

And yet...

Medusa leaned over the table, pointing at a scroll, her voice sharp. "If we destabilize Delphi, Athena's spies will scatter. It gives us room to breathe."

Behind her, Ares chuckled.

"Only you could make espionage sound like foreplay."

She didn't flinch. "Only you could confuse foreplay with strategy."

Hercules entered then, tossing aside his cloak, muscles dusted in the gold of battle. "What's the plan?"

Medusa didn't answer.

She turned.

Eyes slow. Calculating. Dangerous.

"You both think this is about power," she murmured, stepping between them. "But real power?"

She brushed her hand along Ares's jaw. Let it linger.

Then dragged her fingers down Hercules's chest, nails grazing just enough to draw breath.

"Real power," she said, lips at Ares's ear, "is knowing when to use desire to disarm."

"And when not to."

The silence crackled. Neither moved.

Until Ares growled.

"You play with fire."

"And you came here to burn," she said, stepping back with the grace of a queen and the command of a storm.
Later, the war table would hold new marks

strategies etched in ink and memory.

But for now?

It held only breathless tension...

And the echo of three gods learning that seduction

was a political weapon, too.

Chapter One-Hundred-Eighty-Four: The Invitation That Changed Everything

It arrived folded in black silk.

No messenger. No fanfare.

Just a single ribbon marked with Apollo's seal and scented with burnt laurel and starlight.

Medusa didn't open it at first.

She just stared.

Because for all his prophecy and poetry, Apollo didn't beg.

And this?

Felt like begging in silk.

Hades, reading over her shoulder, scowled.

"He's trying to trap you."

"He's trying to warn me," she corrected.

The letter was short.

Just a place. A time.

"Before the next moonrise. Come alone."

No threats.

No flattery.

Just fate.

Ares paced. Hercules gripped his blade.
Andreas watched her with storm-coloured eyes.

"It's dangerous," Hercules said.

"So is staying," Medusa replied.

And that was the truth.

Because something was shifting.

Not just alliances.

The Realms themselves.

So she went.

Alone.

To the forgotten shrine carved beneath the cliffs of Delphi.

Where truth once lived and now barely breathed.

Apollo was waiting.

Not in gold.

Not in light.

But in shadow.

"Why now?" she asked.

"Because I've seen what comes next," he said.
"And I don't want to be on the wrong side of it."

Her breath caught.

"You want to join me?"

"I want to stop being afraid of you."

The silence held like prophecy.

And somewhere...

Fate started rewriting itself.

Chapter One-Hundred-Eighty-Five: The Realignment

Alliances are a currency. And Olympus is bankrupt.

The war council was louder than it had ever been.

Not with shouting.

With silence.

Because Medusa had returned... and Apollo had walked beside her.

Hercules looked ready to punch the sun.

Ares hadn't unsheathed his blade but his knuckles were white from resisting.

Hades stood absolutely still.

"You brought him here," Hades said finally.

"No," Medusa replied. "He brought himself."

Apollo didn't speak.

He didn't need to.

The weight of him standing at Medusa's left side said enough.

And the way Andreas's jaw clenched?

Said the storm brewing wasn't just external.

"Why?" Ares snapped.

Apollo finally lifted his gaze.

"Because I've seen what happens if she stands alone."

"And what happens if she doesn't?" Andreas asked, fire dancing in his fingers.

Apollo's smile didn't reach his eyes.

"Then Olympus falls faster. But at least it will fall to something worthy."

Medusa didn't flinch.

She didn't have to.

This was the moment she'd been building toward.

Where the Realms realigned.

And the gods began to choose.

Not sides.

Futures.

"He'll be useful," Medusa said, voice flat. "Until he isn't."

Apollo inclined his head. "Fair."

And with that, the map changed.

Temples once loyal to Athena turned.

Messages began to fly like arrows.

Whispers filled altars and courtyards.

Because when a god of prophecy shifts his allegiance?

Everyone listens.

Even those who planned to betray you.

Chapter One-Hundred-Eighty-Six: The Betrayer in the Mirror

Not all betrayals are born of hate. Some are born of hunger.

It was past midnight when the mirror whispered.

Not Medusa's mirror.

His.

Andreas stood alone in the eastern chamber, a half-burned scroll in one hand, a memory in the other.

She had said they were safe now.

But Andreas knew better.

He'd grown up in shadows, trained by silence, trusted by no one but her.

And yet

As he stared at the glass, it rippled.

Not with prophecy.

With a face.

His own.

Except it smiled when he didn't.

Moved when he stayed still.

And then it spoke.

"She's already chosen her future," the reflection said.

"It doesn't include you."

Andreas's grip on the scroll tightened.

"You're not real."

"Neither is her promise."

He could feel it then.

Not magic.

Not madness.

Manipulation.

Athena's hand, subtle and sharp, woven through realms like silk through bone.

She was sowing doubt.

But she wasn't done.

Not yet.

Because when Andreas turned from the mirror

He saw someone standing in the doorway.

Apollo.

And the look in his eyes?

Wasn't guilt.

It was regret.

"You weren't supposed to see that," Apollo said.

"And you weren't supposed to be here,"
Andreas growled.

The silence between them was charged.

Not with violence.

With choice.

Because betrayal wasn't always a knife in the
back.

Sometimes, it was a truth offered too late.

And Medusa?

She didn't yet know she was being unravelled from the inside.

Chapter One-Hundred-Eighty-Seven: The Blade Beneath the Crown

Some crowns glitter. Others bleed.

The throne room wasn't built for silence.

It had heard declarations, confessions, threats

But never this.

Medusa sat alone on the obsidian seat, her serpents still, her hands resting gently on the arms of her throne.

She looked like a statue carved from storm and vengeance.

But inside?

She was already bleeding.

Andreas was missing.

Apollo was withholding something.

And Athena's grip on Olympus tightened like a noose made of silk.

She didn't cry.

She calculated.

Because even pain could be a blade if you held it right.

"I know what you're doing," Persephone said from the shadows.

Medusa didn't look at her.

"You think if you slice deep enough, no one will see you bleed," Persephone continued.

"Better than letting them watch me fall," Medusa replied.

Persephone stepped into the light. Her crown gleamed, but her expression was unreadable.

"You're making enemies faster than allies."

"I don't need allies," Medusa said. "I need survivors."

"And what does that make Andreas?"

Medusa finally looked up.

And that was when Persephone knew

She didn't have an answer.

Because Andreas wasn't just a weapon.

He was a wound.

The crown on Medusa's head shimmered.

Not with light.

With fire.

It burned cold, warning the gods in every direction:

You can break her heart.

But you'll never take her throne.

Chapter One-Hundred-Eighty-Eight: The Scream That Echoed Through the Realms

Some screams break sound. Others break destiny.

It started with a breath.

Then a ripple.

Then

The scream.
Not from Medusa.

From the mirror.

Every reflective surface in the palace shattered at once.

Water bowls. Silver trays. Blades. Even the polished marble.

All of them screamed.

A sound that didn't belong in any realm raw, ancient, feminine, and furious.

And it was coming from one place.

The chamber Andreas had vanished from.

Medusa ran.

She didn't hesitate.

Didn't wait for Hades.

Didn't summon Ares.

Didn't explain to Hercules.
She just moved.

Because some grief doesn't knock.

It tears the doors down.

The door to the chamber was open.

Inside

Smoke.

And on the wall, carved into the stone like a curse:

"He was a warning."

Medusa didn't scream.

She didn't collapse.

She stepped forward, into the wreckage.

And stared into the only mirror that hadn't shattered.

It showed her face.

And beside it?

Athena's.

Smiling.

"Let it be war," Medusa whispered, eyes burning green gold.

And the mirror?

Whispered back:

"It already is."

Chapter One-Hundred-Eighty-Nine: When the Gods Finally Chose Sides

Divinity was never neutral. It just pretended longer than most.

The scream had ended.

But its echo lived in the bones of Olympus.

And one by one, the gods began to move.

Not for justice.

Not for loyalty.

But for survival.

Hera was the first.

Not because she loved Medusa.

Not even because she hated Athena.

But because Medusa had once defied Zeus and lived.

"Courage," she said aloud, "is more seductive than order."

Poseidon watched the mirrors ripple and said nothing.

Until a wave crashed unnaturally high on the shores of Olympus.

A silent offering.

And a threat.

Artemis sent no message.

She simply turned her bow away from Medusa's lands.

Sometimes, silence was the loudest allegiance.

But not all turned.

Hermes delivered scrolls to both sides.

He always had.

"Chaos pays well," he whispered, kissing both seals.

And then vanished again.

Dionysus held a feast.

Drank too much.

And painted Medusa's sigil across his chest in wine.

Because sometimes, madness knew exactly where it stood.

And high above it all

Zeus remained in shadow.

Not absent.

Not silent.

Waiting.

Because when gods chose sides?

The sky cracked last.

But hardest.

Chapter One-Hundred-Ninety: The Kiss That Claimed the Storm

Some battles begin with blades. Others begin with lips that taste like war.

The war council had fractured.

Hercules was pacing.

Ares was snarling.

Hades stood silent, every inch of him thunder about to break.

And Medusa?

Medusa watched them all with the patience of a queen and the rage of a woman who had just lost everything.

"Athena took Andreas," she said.

None argued.

"She branded it a warning."

Still, silence.

Medusa stepped closer to the map table, fingers dragging across its carved edges like a blade across skin.

"I am done waiting."

The words split the air.

It was Hades who moved first.
Not to argue.

To stand beside her.

"You have my legions."

Then Hercules.

"My strength."

Then Ares, fire at his fingertips.

"My fury."

But Medusa didn't look at any of them.

She stared at the place on the map marked only by a spiral where the Realms cracked and reality thinned.

"Athena wants fear," she said. "Let's give her fire instead."

Later when the council had broken and war plans bled across every surface

Medusa stood alone on the balcony.

Until Hades joined her.

He didn't speak.

Didn't need to.

She turned.

And kissed him.

Not tender.

Not soft.

Like lightning cleaving sky.

Because this kiss wasn't comfort.

It was promise.

It was war.

And from the shadows, the wind carried her vow

"She will never take from me again."

Interlude: The Crown of Lies (Andreas's POV)

He didn't remember how he got here.

The walls pulsed softly, like a heartbeat golden light, warm and laced with comfort.

Comfort that felt... wrong.

But every time he tried to remember why, the thought slipped sideways.

Like sand through fractured fingers.

He sat on silken sheets, chest bare, wounds gone. Someone had healed him.

Someone kind.

"Andreas."

The voice was a song familiar, soothing.

Athena entered. Not in armour. Not as a general.

But in a gown of pale moonlight, hair down, crown tilted just enough to feel soft instead of sovereign.

"You're safe," she whispered.

He blinked. "Where...?"

"You were betrayed," she said gently, kneeling in front of him.

His breath hitched. Something cracked inside his mind.

"She used you," Athena continued. "Twisted your loyalty. Told you it was love."

"Who...?"

"Medusa."

The name was a thorn.

A word that ached without context.

"She lied," Athena said. "Over and over. Even while you bled for her."

Andreas winced. A memory tried to claw its way back her eyes, her voice, the way she smelled after fire, but it burned. Too bright. Too broken.

"I don't..." His hands shook. "I loved her."

Athena placed her fingers over his heart.

"No. You were enchanted."

He looked up, eyes storm-cloud grey and full of confusion.

"Then why does it still hurt?"

Athena smiled. Not cruelly.

Not yet.

"Because the body remembers," she whispered. "But soon… it won't."

And with a kiss to his forehead, she called the magic down again.

This time, it erased her name from his heart. And replaced it with hers.

Chapter One-Hundred-Ninety-One: The Silence That Wasn't His

The wind didn't howl.

It whispered.

Through the palace halls. Across the broken shrines. Beneath her skin.

Something was wrong.

Not in the obvious way no screaming messengers, no spilled blood or shattered mirrors.

No.

This was worse.

This was quiet.

Medusa stood at the edge of the scrying pool, water still and black, refusing to show her the one face she needed to see.

Andreas.

She had felt his return like a storm coming home.

And now?

Nothing.

Not silence.

Absence.

As if the Realms had swallowed him again only this time, not to hide him...

But to unmake him.

A tremor ran down her spine.

She turned slowly. The others watched her Ares, Hades, Hercules but none spoke.

Because they felt it too.

A ripple in the magic. A thread cut.

He's not dead," she said softly. "I would feel that."

"No," Hades agreed. "But something's severed."

She pressed her hand to her chest.

And winced.

Because where Andreas's magic used to burn like lightning caged in a storm it now felt distant. Faint.

Like an echo that didn't recognize its own voice.

"Athena," she whispered.

It wasn't a guess.

It was a curse.

"She took him again," Medusa said. "But this time…"

Ares stepped closer. "This time she's not keeping him in chains."

"No," Medusa said, eyes narrowing. "She's keeping him in lies."

And as the scrying pool began to shimmer, not with Andreas's face but with Athena's eyes…

Medusa's own magic surged like wildfire.

"She wants war?" she growled. "Then I'll give her a prophecy she won't survive."

Chapter One-Hundred-Ninety-Two: The Oracle Who Wouldn't Lie

Delphi hadn't spoken in days.

No smoke.

No riddles.

No trembling hands guided by divine possession.

Just silence.

Until she came.

The Oracle.

Young. Ancient. Everything between.

Wrapped in veils that whispered secrets even the gods feared to hear.

Medusa didn't kneel.

She didn't have to.

"You've come for a truth you already know," the Oracle said, eyes clouded with stars.

"I've come to hear it from someone who hasn't betrayed me."

The silence that followed wasn't empty it was heavy with everything unsaid.

The Oracle dipped her hand into the blackened pool of prophecy. Ink slithered over her skin like living memory.

"He burns for you," she whispered. "Even now. Even through the veil Athena's woven."

Medusa's breath stilled.

"He remembers?"

"He resists," the Oracle said, "but not for long."

The pool shimmered. A vision flickered:

Andreas, bound in golden thread, lips speaking Athena's name with reverence while his eyes screamed for help.

Medusa gritted her teeth. "She's rewritten him."

The Oracle nodded. "And each time you get close... she rewrites again."

Medusa's fingers curled into fists. "How do I break it?"

The Oracle looked up then eyes burning silver with the weight of fate.

"You don't break a spell like that," she said. "You unwrite it... with something older than magic."

"Like what?"

"Memory. Emotion. The first moment he knew it was you."

Medusa whispered, "The fire."

The Oracle nodded.

"Remind him."

Chapter One-Hundred-Ninety-Three: The God She Thought Was Hers

She expected torment.

She wasn't prepared for seduction.

The cell was cold, carved from stone that hummed with divine silence. Chains hung from the walls not crude metal, but sculpted bands of celestial containment etched with Athena's mark.

Medusa stood in the centre, unbound but caged. Not by steel. By betrayal.

And then... he entered.

Andreas.

No something wearing Andreas's body. The stride was too sure, the smile too cruel, the eyes too clear.

"You," she said, voice rough from days of silence.

He tilted his head. "Me," he echoed. "Improved."

He crossed the chamber without hesitation, boots echoing like a countdown. When he stopped in front of her, Medusa didn't flinch.

But she didn't breathe, either.

"You chose them," he said. "Ares. Hades. Hercules. And left me behind."

"I died for you," she whispered.

"And Athena brought me back. Not as your shadow. As her blade."

He reached for her. Not to strike but to cradle her jaw.

And she let him.

Until his thumb dragged across her bottom lip, and his voice dipped into dangerous desire.

"I still remember what you taste like."

Medusa's heart stuttered.

"But now," he continued, leaning in until breath mingled, "I know what power tastes like too. And you... you're no longer my queen."

His mouth claimed hers.

It wasn't gentle.

It was a test. A taunt. A final echo of what they once were.

And gods help her

For a breathless second, she kissed him back.

Then bit his lip hard enough to taste metal.

"You'll regret this," she said.

He laughed, blood at the corner of his smile.
"Only if you stop being fun."

Then he left her in the dark.

With chains she couldn't see.

And the truth she couldn't un-feel.

Interlude: The War Beneath Her Smile

Athena's Point of View

They always underestimated intelligence.

Give them blood, give them brute force, and the gods would cheer.

But give them strategy give them a woman who built empires in silence, and they'd call it manipulation.

Let them.

Athena stood above the reflecting pool in her private chamber; a thousand glowing threads of fate tangled in the air before her. Each one connected to a decision. A betrayal. A god. A queen.

Medusa.

She touched the thread bearing her name.

Not to cut it.

To tighten it.

"She thinks she still has allies," Athena murmured, watching an illusion of Medusa pace in her cell. "She thinks love will save her."

The word tasted sour.

Love.

The thing that had softened empires.

Weakened queens.

Ruined gods.

Athena had no use for it.

She preferred devotion.

And Andreas?

He was very, very devoted.

She turned to the corner of the chamber where he now knelt, silent, still his eyes empty of everything but purpose.

Her purpose.

"I gave you back your mind," she said softly. "And in return, you will end hers."

Andreas didn't respond.

He didn't need to.

The spell etched into his spine laced with forgotten tongues and divine command responded for him.

Athena smiled.

Not the brittle smile of diplomacy.

The cruel curve of certainty.

"Let her rage," she whispered. "Let her plot and scream and think she still holds the board."

She reached out to the pool again.

And this time, she didn't just touch Medusa's thread.

She braided it with Andreas's.

And pulled.

Interlude: The Silence That Refused to Break

The chains didn't rattle.

They didn't need to.

Silence was a better prison.

No screams. No spells. No swords.

Just breath. And stone. And the echo of lips that once swore love now laced with power that wasn't hers.

Medusa sat in the centre of the chamber. Not collapsed. Not caged.

Coiled.

She hadn't moved since Andreas left. Not because she was defeated.

Because she was remembering.

Every promise broken.

Every betrayal kissed into her skin.

Every god who thought fire only burned in men.

They were wrong.

Fire lived in silence, too.

In the stillness before storms.

In queens who watched.

In women who waited.

Not to be saved.

To rise.

A faint breeze stirred the ends of her serpents.

She didn't look up.

But her eyes flickered.

And the realm trembled.

Chapter One-Hundred-Ninety-Four: The Queen Who Refused to Break

Chains couldn't hold what they couldn't understand.

Medusa had been silent for three days.

Not broken. Not bowed.

Becoming.

Every god watching her cell whether through mirror, magic, or mortal means saw stillness and assumed surrender.

But inside?

She was gathering.

Her power. Her pain. Her purpose.

Andreas 's betrayal didn't shatter her.

It sharpened her.

The room whispered. Not with words, but with memory. Each carved stone, each etched curse on the walls they hummed with divine spite. But Medusa had lived through worse.

Had become worse.

And now she waited.

Not for rescue.

For resonance.

It came with a tremor. A crack in the silence so thin it could have been a dream.

But she felt it.

Her serpents stirred.

A voice faint and furious called through the realms.

Not Ares. Not Hades. Not Hercules.

A woman.

A goddess.

"Hold," the voice whispered.

And Medusa did.

She stood.

The chains didn't stop her.

They shattered.

She walked through the threshold of her prison not saved, not stolen.

Awakened.

Because queens weren't freed.

They freed themselves.

Chapter One-Hundred-Ninety-Five: The Reckoning Crowned in Fire

The halls of Olympus had never felt this quiet.

Not after war. Not after prophecy. But after her return.

Medusa didn't storm the gates. She walked. Alone. Crowned not in gold but in silence and every god could feel it.

Behind her, the air shimmered with those who followed: titans reborn in oath, minor gods burned by betrayal, and her lovers Ares, Hercules, and Hades no longer divided in purpose.

The queen had returned.

Athena stood at the apex of the throne room, flanked by Apollo and a Andreas that was no longer hers.

Medusa met his gaze once and didn't look away.

"Where is your leash, Andreas?" she asked coldly. "Or did Athena finally let you think for yourself?"

His jaw clenched, but he didn't speak.

Athena stepped forward, calm as marble. "You walk into your death."

"I walk into your judgment," Medusa replied. "You used to stand for wisdom. Now you hide behind puppets and fear."

"You call this fear?" Athena asked, gesturing around. "You are one woman."

"I am a thousand choices you tried to silence," Medusa said. "And I brought every one of them with me."

Behind her, the torches blazed to life.

The Realms had answered.

And Olympus was about to burn.

Chapter One-Hundred-Ninety-Six: The Gods Who Chose Fire

Olympus was no longer silent.

It roared.

Flames licked the marble columns like lovers reunited. Smoke curled in divine patterns through the vaulted halls as gods and monsters, rebels and remnants surged forward behind the queen who refused to bow.

Medusa.

She didn't run.

She didn't shout.

She walked.

Every step echoed like a declaration, her serpents rising with regal fury. Her eyes met each challenge without hesitation, her power uncoiling around her like prophecy itself.

Athena stood unmoved at the throne.

But she was not untouched.

Andreas flanked her still, a sword drawn, but something flickered in his gaze. Memory? Madness? A crack in the spell?

It didn't matter.

Not yet.

Medusa stopped halfway up the stairs, the ruined council floor beneath her feet. Her voice, when it came, was not loud.

But it didn't need to be.

"You tried to erase me."

A pause. The weight of centuries in her tone.

"And like all fools who fear women crowned in pain, you forgot what grows in silence."

Athena's lips curled into a blade-thin smile. "Ruin."

"Revolution," Medusa corrected.

Then the gods moved.

Ares launched first, fire in his hands and fury in his heart.

Hercules followed, a shield of legend breaking through Athena's summoned phalanx.

And Hades?

He did not rush.

He vanished and reappeared in shadows behind Andreas.

"You're not hers," Hades whispered into Andreas's ear.

Andreas swung.

Hades caught the blade in one palm. Blood ran. He didn't flinch.

"Remember who you bled for."

Medusa met Athena on the steps, blades crossing, the crown glowing between them.

"This is not vengeance," she said.

"No," Athena hissed. "It's war."

Their clash shattered the marble beneath them.

The war for Olympus had begun.

And the gods?

They chose fire.

Chapter One-Hundred-Ninety-Seven: The Fire That Would Not Bow

The aftermath tasted like ash and divinity.

Olympus burned behind her, columns cracked, banners torn, and the scent of gods' fear thick in the air. But Medusa did not pause to admire the wreckage.

She was not here to win.

She was here to end it.

Behind her, Ares limped slightly, one arm slick with ichor. Hercules leaned on his shield like it was the only thing holding him upright. Hades moved like a shadow stitched from vengeance.

And Andreas?

Andreas knelt.

Not in surrender. In torment.

The spell had cracked. His memories flooded back, jagged and cruel, pieces of a life Athena had tried to erase. He looked up at Medusa, eyes bleeding regret.

"I didn't choose this," he whispered.

She stared down at him. "No," she agreed. "But you didn't fight it either."

He didn't argue.

Didn't beg.

That, at least, he remembered.

"I'll make it right," he said.

Medusa turned away. "Start by getting out of my way."

She passed him.

Not cruel.

Not kind.

A queen with a war still raging in her chest.

At the steps of the shattered throne, Athena was gone. Not dead. Not defeated. Just vanished.

And Medusa knew it wasn't over.

Not yet.

The Realms still trembled. The gods still watched.

And the crown?

It no longer needed a throne.

It followed her.

Chapter One-Hundred-Ninety-Eight: The Silence Before Storms

The skies above Olympus didn't clear.

They simmered.

Clouds thick with divine residue swirled like judgment held back, and the wind whispered names only gods would dare forget.

Medusa stood at the cliff's edge where marble met the sky.

No throne behind her.

No chains before her.

Just power waiting to be wielded.

Ares approached first, one hand bandaged, the other holding a flask of something too ancient to name.

"You should rest."

"I should rebuild," she said.

Hercules came next. He dropped a cracked piece of his own armour beside her like an offering.

"If Olympus doesn't fall completely, it'll retaliate."

"It already has," she murmured. "It sent Andreas."

Silence.

Then Hades appeared, his presence colder than the air that trembled at his arrival.

"Athena is not finished," he said. "She's wounded. Not dead. That makes her dangerous."

Medusa didn't flinch. Her gaze stayed on the horizon.

"Let her come."

"You want her to," Hades said, voice a quiet accusation.

"I want her to see what happens when you corner the wrong woman."

The wind caught her words and carried them into the clouds.

Lightning answered.

Behind her, the three gods stood in shadow.

But in front of her?

A realm reshaped.

Not by peace.

By reckoning.

Because some storms didn't scream when they came.

Some came in silence.

And then shattered everything.

Chapter One-Hundred-Ninety-Nine: The Throne That Waited

The crown sat where no god dared place it.

Not on the throne.

But on the stone beneath it.

Where battles had bled. Where oaths had broken.

Where Medusa now stood.

She didn't reach for it.

Not yet.

The Realms had quieted just enough to breathe, not enough to rest.

Hercules stood at her right, still bleeding beneath his grin.

Ares guarded her back, restless, ready, radiating heat like a warning.

And Hades?

He watched the shadows.

Because not all enemies wore crowns.

Andreas remained behind. Not kneeling. Not forgiven.

But no longer lost.

And above them, Olympus didn't crumble.

It waited.

"Take it," Ares said.

Medusa didn't move.

"She already has," Hades answered.

And that was true.

Because the crown was no longer an object.

It was a symbol.

A prophecy fulfilled not by inheritance but by endurance.

She stepped forward.

Not to be queen.

To redefine what it meant.

As her fingers closed around the metal, the Realms shifted.

Not with fear.

With faith.

The throne would never hold her.

Because she was never meant to sit.

She was meant to rise

And the gods?

Would rise with her.

Interlude: What Fire Remembers

The embers hadn't cooled.

Not in Olympus.

Not in her chest.

Medusa stood at the edge of a shattered balcony, the wind combing through her serpents like a memory that refused to fade.

She wasn't thinking of Athena.

She wasn't even thinking of Andreas.

She was remembering the first fire

The one that burned in silence.

The one that made her a monster.

The one no god ever apologized for.

"You were always too loud," they had said.

"Too powerful."

"Too much."

But fire doesn't forget.

And Medusa didn't forgive.

Behind her, footsteps approached.

Hades. Ares. Hercules.

None spoke.

They didn't need to.

They stood beside her, shoulder to shoulder,
letting the silence say what gods never could:

You were never too much.

You were the match they should never have lit.

And now?

Now the Realms would burn for what they tried
to bury.

Chapter Two-Hundred: The Throne That Didn't Need Permission

The shattered throne room was quiet.

Not empty never empty but quiet in the way temples hold their breath before a storm.

Medusa stood where Athena once ruled, not seated but cantered. The throne behind her was broken, a jagged ruin of divine arrogance and marble pride.

She didn't fix it.

She didn't need to.

A queen did not require permission from a chair to rule.

Her crown glowed faintly not gold, not forged, but earned. Fire kissed the tips of her serpents, and the Realms shimmered with a new kind of balance: not peace, not victory, but reckoning.

The gods came.

Not all.

But enough.

Some out of loyalty.

Some out of curiosity.

Some just to see if the girl with the cursed gaze had truly won.

She hadn't.

Not in the way they expected.

She'd survived.

She'd endured.

And in doing so, she'd become something Olympus had no word for.

Not goddess.

Not monster.

Not queen.

Something older.

Something that didn't need a title to command fear, or a throne to claim power.

When Andreas stepped into the hall, still bleeding regret, still echoing betrayal, she didn't look away.

Neither did he.

"You're not the same," he said quietly.

"Neither are you."

They didn't embrace.

Didn't fight.

They just... stood.

Two histories tangled in one aftermath.

Ares moved beside her. Hercules behind.
Hades in shadow. All of them ready.

And yet she raised no blade.

Because Olympus didn't need more blood.
It needed truth.

And Medusa was done asking permission to
speak it.

Chapter Two-Hundred-One: The Crown That Chose Her

The halls of Olympus had never seen a night like this.

Not when kings rose.

Not when empires fell.

But tonight, the throne room pulsed with power raw, divine, undeniable as Medusa stepped into the light not as a contender...

But as a queen.

The flames that once danced in rebellion now roared in tribute. Gods, titans, exiles, and shadows lined the golden steps of the court. The sky above cracked with celestial lightning, and the floor beneath her heels shimmered with enchantments only the old gods remembered.

Hades stood to the left.

Ares to the right.

Hercules just behind her, still blood-marked from battle, but unyielding in loyalty.

And Andreas?

He watched from the shadows, unhealed and uncertain, unable to look away.

Medusa wore no gown.

She wore armour sleek, obsidian-black, etched with silver serpents and woven prophecy. Her crown was not placed. It formed. From power. From purpose. From every moment she had been underestimated and refused to kneel.

It hovered a second above her head,
shimmering with divine heat then lowered.

Like Olympus itself bowed.

A hush fell.

Even the stars outside paused their spin.

Then a voice boomed, neither male nor female.
Neither old nor new.

"All hail the crowned flame."

Gasps echoed.

Her crown ignited.

Gold to fire. Fire to light. Light to prophecy.

Ares knelt first.

Hades followed.

Then Hercules.

Then every being present one by one, realm by realm.

Not for fear.

For fire.

The fire she had become.

Medusa didn't smile.

She didn't need to.

The crown did it for her.

Interlude: The Night Olympus Bowed (And She Didn't Sleep Alone)

The crown was still warm.

It sat on the edge of the bed forgotten, for once its gold eclipsed by the heat rising in the room.

Medusa stood at the window, bare shoulders kissed by moonlight, her newly claimed realm stretching beneath her like a held breath. Behind her, the door opened.

And closed.

She didn't turn.

"You're late," she said.

Ares chuckled first. "We thought you'd want a moment to yourself."

"I've had centuries of moments."

"And now?" Hades asked, stepping into the dark like it belonged to him.

"Now," she murmured, turning, "I want to remember what power tastes like when it's mine."

Hercules was the first to cross the space. He kissed her like she was a war he'd already lost and was glad for it. Her hands traced his scars, his jaw, the promises he didn't say out loud.

Then Ares was there fiery, rough, impatient as ever. He bit her lower lip and growled into her mouth, "You wore that crown like sin incarnate."

"It wasn't for you," she whispered.

He smirked. "Still enjoyed the view."

And Hades gods, Hades, he didn't touch her at first. He just watched. Silent. Reverent. Until she crooked a finger and said, "I'm not a goddess you can worship from afar."

He moved like night and claimed her like a secret.

Their bodies tangled in silk and shadows, a worship of heat and hunger. No thrones. No war. Just sweat and sound and surrender.

Medusa didn't kneel.

But they did.

One by one.

Because this night wasn't about crowns or kingdoms.

It was about a woman who rose from ruin

And reminded the gods why they had always feared her fire.

Chapter Two-Hundred-Two: The Gods Who Still Watched

The crown was no longer a question.

It was law.

Medusa stood on the obsidian balcony of the temple that now bore her name, high above the molten veins of Olympus, where the stars themselves bent in deference. Wind tugged at her silks, darker now, threaded with the gold of prophecy and the red of victory.

But she didn't feel victorious.

She felt... watched.

Not by mortals. Not by gods.

By something older.

By the Realms themselves.

"They're quiet," she murmured, arms resting along the edge of the balcony. "Too quiet."

Behind her, Hades moved. Barefoot. Silent. A shadow stitched into form.

"They wait," he said. "The balance has shifted. When it does, the old powers stir."

Ares leaned against the archway, his armor undone, his temper not. "Let them stir. I'll make them kneel."

"You always say that," Hercules replied as he entered, a single golden olive branch in his hand, Athena's former symbol, now snapped in two.

"And I always do," Ares shot back.

But Medusa didn't turn.

Not yet.

Because far beneath the peaks of Olympus, in temples no longer mapped, the ground was glowing.

Not fire.

Not magic.

Summoning.

Andreas had felt it first.

He hadn't spoken of it. But Medusa had seen it, in the way his hands trembled when touching old stone, the way he stared too long at the mirrors that no longer showed reflections.

He was cracking.

Again.

Only this time, it wasn't Athena.

It was something far worse.

Something forgotten.

"Something's coming," she whispered.

Hades didn't argue.

Neither did the others.

Because in the quiet after a storm, only fools
believed peace would last.

The gods were shifting.

And the Realms?

They were watching.

Interlude: The God Who Chose Wrong

The stars did not weep for Andreas.

They only watched.

Cold. Eternal. Unforgiving.

He stood at the edge of Olympus, where the winds cut like truth and the past echoed in every stone. The battle was over. The crown had chosen.

But not him.

He had bent once to power, let Athena remake him in the image of a weapon, not a man. And though the spell had broken... the fracture remained.

He remembered everything.

And yet... part of him still *missed it*.

The clarity. The cruelty. The *purpose. *

He hadn't told Medusa everything.

Not the part where Athena hadn't needed chains to control him. Not the part where, even now, some dark thread still tugged at his loyalty not out of magic, but temptation.

"I could have been a god beside her," he whispered to the void.

But the wind didn't answer.

Only the distant echo of Medusa's coronation song, one he had not been invited to.

The Realms had crowned their queen.

And Andreas?

Andreas had chosen wrong.

Chapter Two-Hundred-Three: The Queen Returns Too Late

Medusa felt it before she saw it.

A tear in the sky thin, dark, and humming with the sound of rewritten fate.

The coronation was barely behind her. Her lovers still slept in the tangled heat of victory. Her people still danced in the light of their first free dawn.

But the sky...

It cracked.

From the rift stepped a figure not draped in wisdom, but in shadow.

Athena.

But changed.

Her golden armour was gone. Replaced with something older stitched from threads of forgotten fear, edged in secrets too deep for daylight.

Her crown?

Forged from *memory lost* and *mercy refused*.

Behind her... a legion.

Not gods. Not mortals. Something in between. Twisted. Beautiful. Terrifying.

Medusa summoned her power, but the earth did not answer as quickly as before. The crown shimmered uncertainly.

She was queen.

But this was no longer Olympus.

This was something else.

"Athena," Medusa breathed.

The goddess smiled. "You thought I was gone?"

"You lost."

"I evolved."

And when their eyes met

the Realms trembled.
Again.

Because the war hadn't ended.

It had just *begun again*.

And this time?

Medusa might have returned too late.

Sneak Peek – Book Four: Divine Submission – The Throne of Ruin

The crown still shimmered on her head, but the throne was already ash.

Andreas stood at Athena's side unflinching, unforgiven his soul rewritten in silence.

And Medusa?

She was too late to stop the gods who whispered in shadows, too late to undo the choice that shattered Olympus in secret.

The war wasn't over.

It had only changed shape.

And this time, the divine wouldn't battle for power.

They would battle for truth.

Even if it meant crowning a villain.

Letter from Medusa

Epilogue to Book Three: Divine Submission –

The Realm of Echoes

To the one still watching,

I was never the villain of this story.

Nor the victim.

I was the girl they tried to erase.

The woman they feared too loudly.

The queen they never saw coming.

They wrote my name in whispers,

scrawled it in warnings,

etched it into temple walls beside monsters.

But I remember who I was before the curse.

Before the gods turned me into myth.

And I remember who I became because of it.

You think this story ends here with a crown, a kiss, a war paused just long enough to breathe?

No.

This is the breath before the fire.

Because the real war was never just Olympus. It was the lie they made of me. The rewriting of women who dared to rise. The punishment for love turned powerful.

I loved.

Oh, gods, I loved.

I loved a man made of shadows.

A warrior forged in blood.

A god who swore his heart before his blade.

And once, I loved a boy with storm-coloured eyes

Until he became the storm itself.

But I will not break for him again.

I am not ash. I am not ruin.

I am rebirth.

And when Athena returns with her crown of darker power,

when Andreas stands at her side, torn or twisted

I will not beg.

I will not falter.

I will stand.

Crowned.

Commanding.

And ready.

So, if you're still watching... hold your breath.

The next chapter isn't peace.

It's reckoning.

- M.

Character Index – The Divine Submission Series

Medusa

The central heroine. Once betrayed and transformed, now a crowned queen defying Olympus. Fierce, strategic, and unapologetically powerful.

Andreas

Medusa's former mortal lover, twisted by Athena into a loyal weapon. Torn between love and control. A tragic thread through the series.

Ares

God of War. One of Medusa's fiercest protectors and lovers. Hot-headed, bold, loyal and burns with desire and rage in equal measure.

Hades

God of the Underworld. Cold and calculating but fiercely devoted to Medusa. Their connection is built on shared pain and raw understanding.

Hercules

Champion of strength and legend. Loyal, passionate, and surprisingly tender. Shares a steamy and emotional bond with Medusa.

Athena

Goddess of Wisdom and Medusa's greatest enemy. Ruthless, controlling, and feared. Manipulates memory, loyalty, and legacy.

Apollo

God of prophecy and light. Torn between sides. Fascinated by Medusa's rise and shaken by his own doubts.

Persephone

Queen of the Underworld. Politically calculating. At odds with Medusa's claim to power and throne.

Echo form Aurelya

Medusa's counterpart from the Realm of Echoes. A symbol of reflection, memory, and the path not taken.

Aurelya / Arexia

The Crowned Flame / The Echoed Crown

Aurelya is the goddess who rose through prophecy, sacrifice, and love. Fire incarnate, she is a queen forged not by bloodline, but by breaking the chains that bound her. With serpents for secrets and thrones turned to ash, she walked through divine trials to reclaim her name and her crown.

But in the Mirror of the Realms, something else watched.

Arexia is her echo an unbroken version, forged in power, untouched by mercy. Cold fire. Precision without pity. A queen crowned in what Aurelya chose to leave behind. A reflection, perhaps.

Or something far more dangerous.

The Realms

Sentient planes of existence influenced by emotion, memory, and divine will. Each has rules, and some are breaking.

Realms and Magical Creatures Index

Realms of Divine Submission

Olympus

The seat of divine politics and the battleground of gods. Power, betrayal, and legacy pulse through its marble halls.

The Underworld

Hades' shadowed dominion, full of secrets, memory rivers, and truth that can't be outrun.

The Mortal Realm

Once a place of prophecy and consequence, now warped by divine games. Mortals are pawns, prophets, or forgotten.

The Mirror Realms

Fractured, warped reflections of reality. Where alternate choices become twisted realities. Dangerous, seductive, and ever shifting.

The Realm of Echoes

A haunting realm where past and possibility whisper. Echo form gods are born here, shaped by memory and unfinished fate.

Magical Creatures

Serpent-Crown Familiars

Medusa's snakes are not mere adornments, they are extensions of her power, emotions, and prophecy.

Cerberan Wraiths

Guardians of Underworld secrets. Three-headed spectral beasts bound to Hades' will, called only in times of true crisis.

Mirror Wyrms

Slithering dragons of the Mirror Realms. They feast on memory and coil around regret.

Phoenix of Reckoning

Once per age, this divine firebird rises at the fall of empires. Said to choose the next queen or burn her.

Oracle Moths

Silver-winged insects that whisper forgotten futures. Found only where fate unravels.

Post-Credit Chapter: The One Who Watched Back

The Realm of Echoes did not slumber.

Beneath the last breath of prophecy, beyond the fires of Olympus and the roots of Yggdrasil, the mirror still pulsed.

It had witnessed crowns rise. Lovers fall. Fates fracture and gods burn for the woman who refused to kneel.

Now, it shimmered again not with memory, but invitation.

Medusa stood before it, alone this time. No throne. No serpents whispering. Just her reflection. Except

It wasn't her.

Not exactly.

The woman in the glass wore her face, but colder. Sharper. Her lips curved in a smirk that never reached her eyes. She stood taller not in height, but in presence. Regal. Ruthless. Radiant in a way that threatened to devour the room.

Her serpents were still, coiled in golden rings like a crown of order. Her dress was ash-silk. Her eyes? Starless.

And she was not waiting to be summoned.

"You," Medusa whispered, throat tight. "I've seen you before..."

The reflection tilted her head.

"You've seen parts of me," she said. "But you still think I'm your shadow. Your future. You're warning."

She stepped forward. The mirror didn't shatter.

It opened.

"I am not you, Medusa," the woman said, stepping out with sovereign stillness. "I'm what was left behind when you chose love."

The air around her bent. The Realms themselves listened.

"I am the version that never needed to be broken to become divine."

"Then what are you?" Medusa asked, the weight of a thousand gods thrumming in her chest.

The woman smiled.

"I am Arexia," she said. "The Rewrite You Buried. The Crown You Refused. The Echo That Watched While You Burned."

She turned, and as she walked back through the mirror no longer a reflection but a gate, she left three words behind that curled like prophecy in Medusa's bones:

"She's coming next."

About the Author

Holly Symons writes dangerously seductive tales where goddesses wear crowns, gods fall to their knees, and power is the greatest foreplay.

She is the creator of the Realmsverse an epic fantasy universe where mythology gets rewritten, one steamy chapter at a time.

When she's not conjuring chaos between queens and gods, Holly is dreaming up new rebellions, new Realms, and even more divine submission.